WAHIDA CLARK PRESENTS

THUGS

7

RAW & UNCUT
~ PREVIEW ~
with special bonus inside

Wahida Clark

NEW YORK TIMES BESTSELLING AUTHOR

AUG - - 2018

WAHIDA CLARK PRESENTS

Thugs 7: Raw & Uncut Preview

By
Wahida Clark

Thugs 7: Raw & Uncut Preview

This is a work of fiction. Names, characters, places, and incidents either are the product of the author's imagination or are used fictitiously, and any resemblance to actual persons, living or dead, business establishments, events, or locales are entirely coincidental.

Wahida Clark Presents Publishing
60 Evergreen Place Suite 904-A
Suite 904A
East Orange, New Jersey 07018
1(866)-910-6920

www.wclarkpublishing.com

Library of Congress Cataloging-In-Publication Data:

ISBN 13-digit 978-1-9449926-1-3 (paperback)
ISBN 13-digit 978-919449926-0-6 (ebook)

1. New York, NY- 2. Drug Trafficking- 3. African Americans-Fiction- 4. Urban Fiction- 5. Robbery- 6. Every Thug Needs A Lady

Cover design and layout by Nuance Art, LLC
Book design by NuanceArt@aCreativeNuance.com
Edited by Linda Wilson

Printed in USA

Table of Contents

Sneak Peak

Chapter One

Rick

"Are you going to let me in or what?" I pleaded through the screen door that separated me from Kyra, my soon-to-be baby's mama in which I soon will have two. Kyra is seven months and Nina is almost nine. Even though Tasha and the kids went back to New York, Kyra and Marva, Tasha's aunt, remained at the Southern California home. I had been knocking on Kyra's door for five minutes now. Each knock getting louder by the pound. "What the fuck?" I mumbled to myself. She knew I was coming. I sent her a text right before my flight from Phoenix to Cali. Now I'm ringing her phone and banging on the window. I'm about to bust this muthafucka in.

Suddenly the blinds flew up. "What do you want, Rick?"

What the fuck do she mean what do I want? This wasn't a surprise visit. "I want to see you. See how you're doing. Do you need anything? Kyra, please. I'm just trying to talk to you to see how we gonna work this out."

Kyra sighed and shook her head. I obviously said the wrong shit. But it was too late. Two things you can't take back, and that's spoken words and arrows. Once they're gone, they're gone.

"Of this, Rick? I mean, really? Of this? What exactly do

7

you mean?"

"Kyra, you know what the fuck I mean."

"Oh, do I?" If looks could kill, I would be dead. "*This?* Do you mean *this?*" She pointed at her stomach. "*This* baby will be here in two months and you still haven't left that bitch, so no need to worry about *this*." She pointed at her stomach again, and then closed the blinds.

"How long do I have to wait before you stop acting like this?" I knew she was within earshot.

"As long as it takes for you to leave her."

"Kyra, I told you. Both of you knew what time it was. I told y'all up front that I am *not* leaving her. And I told her that I'm *not* leaving you. I didn't lie to y'all. So, both of y'all are going to have to deal with it. I love both of you. Y'all are carrying my babies, and I damn sure ain't letting y'all's silliness stop my babies from growing up together. I don't know how or when you will come to grips with things, but you need to do so soon. As you stated, you only have two months. So, in two months we will be one big happy family."

Kyra never opened the door.

Kyra

Rick was banging on the door and ringing the doorbell and blowing up my cell phone like a madman causing my stomach to become hard as a rock. I guess my baby could sense the tension. I didn't care. I glared at him when I raised the blinds and in that moment, I was getting weak. I wanted to open the door and jump into his arms. But my pride

8

wouldn't let me do it.

It was my pride that urged me to be angry and act like a spoiled brat. My pride talked me into missing one of the best parts of being pregnant, in my opinion. Tasha calls it getting pregnant-spoiled by your man. But I can't claim him as my man, even though he wants me to. He is still with her. They have a family, and she's pregnant too. He even had the nerve to ask me to move to Arizona. If he had his way, we would all be living in the same house. Go figure out that bullshit! The thought of him being with her burns me the fuck up.

I covered my ears to block out hearing him call my name and to resist the urge to open the door, take him upstairs, and fuck the shit out of him. And on the other hand, blow his fucking brains out. I love him to death, but Lord knows I do *not* want to be no side baby mama. That shit is crazy.

"Mom! Mom!" Aisha, my eight-year-old daughter, was calling me. "You said you was going to let him in this time!" Her friendly reminder not warranted. Yes, I did tell her that, but like I said, my pride wouldn't allow me to do it. "You do this every time! You have no discipline." She turned and stomped away.

"Aisha! Aisha! Get your little behind back here! What did you say to me?" I dared her with my expression to repeat what she just said. All of this anger I have built up inside for Rick is threatening to come out at my daughter.

She was now standing right in front of me. My baby has been through so much. She lost me, when I was in a coma. Then she lost Marvin, her dad, a conversation that we continue to have. I honestly don't know how to deal with her. I wish I would have taken Tasha up on her offer and let her go to New York.

"I'm sorry, Mom. But you said you was going to let him in the next time he came by, and then we were going to all go out. This is getting old, Mom."

"What do you know about something getting old? You better hope you *live* to be old, popping off your mouth at me like that. You're supposed to be on *my* side, Aisha."

"I am, Ma, but dang."

No, this child *isn't* talking to me like this. I was trying my best not to laugh.

"Dang what, Aisha? What do you want me to do?"

"I want you to walk over to the door and open it just like this."

"Aisha, no!" I stopped her just in time.

Jaz

I stood on the porch watching the eighteen-wheeler backing into the driveway. Here we were back in Jersey again. I didn't know whether to celebrate or cry when we decided on East Rutherford, to be exact. If it was up to me, I would have never left Georgia to come where the winters are filled with snow. But Faheem had the final say, and Kaeerah was going with whatever her father said.

We all were still grieving the loss of li'l Faheem being gone. No parent should ever have to bury their child or children. His dad was doing his best dealing with the reality.

He still had his moments. I would catch him now and then staring off into space or getting quiet in the middle of conversations, and other times, he would pick up his Qur'an and read for hours nonstop. Those were the times that I think he would be reflecting on his son the most. But, I can only assume that my assumptions are right because he refuses to talk about it with me. Since I am not his son's birth mother, I think Faheem feels that there is a disconnect, which is not true. I know that eventually he will be fine.

When Kaeerah asked him how long she was supposed to feel sad that her brother wasn't coming back, he simply told her, "Until you choose to be happy. No one comes in this world or leaves without Allah's permission, and stop feeling sad." He then told her that Allah would bless her with another baby brother, and he looked over at me. That's when I got up and walked out of the room. Now is not the right time to have a baby.

Angel

I was superexcited that my girls Tasha and Jaz were back on the East Coast. I snapped my fingers doing my chair dance. And since Kaylin gave me two weeks away from the office, I was free to celebrate, spend time with my girls, and most importantly . . . shopppppp! My favorite hobby. Thanks to Zaddy Kaylin, I was also looking forward to the kids getting together. Am I getting old thinking of play dates? Am I *really* trading in popping bottles for picnics? Nahhhh. Never that. I will be a fly bitch until the end of time.

11

I remember when we were all single with no kids; now, we almost have a village. And since Tasha and Kyra both were seven months, I figured I'd use that as an excuse and my theme for my get-together and to throw a double baby shower. I loved throwing parties. Hell, my plan was to put on a shower that was going to shut social media down. I even had a filter created for the day. And so far, my family gathering/baby shower was coming together flawlessly.

The only, only thing I saw tainting my event was inviting Rick. Kyra said she would come but made me promise and swear that I wouldn't invite Rick. Y'all know me. I couldn't do that.

Lost. We were all still healing over our losses. Both, my brother and my sister, Carmen, were murdered. Tasha lost her cousin Stephon, and then her sister, Trina. Jaz lost her sister and li'l Faheem. Kyra lost Marvin. Trae lost his cousin. Kaylin lost Kyron. I mean, damn. I think we owed it to ourselves to celebrate life. And what better way than with a baby shower? With all of the Ls we took, if we didn't have babies on the way, we *still* needed to see each other and love one another. This was my only family.

Kaylin

I had to pat myself on the back. Everything was going as planned, and I couldn't wait to reveal my surprises. Angel was happy. She now had a legitimate excuse to spend my money. But seriously, she really wanted to spend time with her girls, so she flew Kyra in, using the double baby shower as the excuse. We even made sure Rick, against Kyra's wishes, found his way to take part in the festivities, even though he didn't look like he was having a good time. Kyra was obviously giving him the blues. Y'all sisters can be so relentless, unyielding, and unforgiving over shit a nigga did. *Damn.*

I finally got Angel's attention, a.k.a. Red, and signaled for her to meet me in the kitchen. As soon as she walked through, I grabbed her up.

"Bae, what's up?" She looked at me skeptically.

I pulled her close and kissed her on the neck and began easing her toward the stairs. "Watching you work the room in this dress, well, um, I think you can pretty much *feel* what I'm up to." I had her at the steps.

"Kaylin, no."

"Why do women always gotta say no?" I was making sure she knew my dick was hard.

"Not. Now. Kaylin." She tried to squirm away, but her wiggling on my dick was only getting me harder.

"We are *not* going upstairs. So, bae, not right now. There are too many people walking around." She was giggling.

"Who said anything about going upstairs? I just need you to bend over a couple of these steps." I was able to maneuver one of my hands in between her thighs.

"Kaylin . . . Baby, later."

"What? I only want a kiss."

"Stop lying, Kaylin."

"Just a kiss." I lifted her up and began walking up the

stairs. She held her arms out, palms pressing against both sides of the walls of the back, narrow stairwell in an attempt to stop me. But all that did was put her in the position I needed her to be in. I now had ahold of her clit, and I wasn't letting go.

"Kaylin, somebody is going to come." She could barely speak.

"You are." I had unzipped my pants and released my bone.

"Somebody is going to come, baby."

"Shhhhhhhhh. I got this." I was now trying to go up inside of her.

"Kaylin, we got . . . *companeeee*. Oh shit," she muttered as she began to ride my dick. I just wanted to get up in the pussy for a few minutes.

"Ayo! Red, you feel so good, baby." She was riding up and down and was already trembling. She was trying to hurry and get her nut off before someone came. Pun intended!

We both came almost at the same time.

"See. I told you I only needed a minute."

"That was two. Two good minutes. *Really* good minutes, bae. I love you." She then kissed me like she meant it. Nothing like sneaking and freaking with the thought of getting caught. My kind of midday fuck!

"See, and you almost missed that." I slid her dress back over her ass, just in time. I heard voices right behind us as I put my shit away. My cell rang. "Go on back to your party. I'll get with you later. I gotta make that run."

"Can't wait, big daddy." She kissed me on the lips, turned

14

around, and went up the stairs. I glanced at the caller ID. Mari. I let it go to voice mail.

Tasha

This is the unhappiest time of my life. Trae is still locked up way across the damn country. He's been gone now for 297 days. But who's counting? To make matters worse, I haven't seen or heard from him in almost a month. I'm praying that while he's sitting in that cell, he's focused on getting his ass home to his family instead of Kyron fucking me. You know how it is with nothing but time on your hands, you think of all kinds of bullshit. But . . . If I could take it back, I wouldn't. He deserved every stroke that nigga made inside of his wife's pussy. That's how deep my anger ran. He forgot the vows we made, and I had to show him that two can play that game.

Anyways, I'm back here in New York with the kids in our tiny-ass apartment. The walls are closing in on me. I hate New York. This pregnancy is nothing like the first two. I've gained almost forty-five pounds. The kids are driving me crazy. They want and need their father. Every day they ask when is he coming home. I mean, this is beginning to be a bit much. And now, Angel gets this brilliant idea to throw a baby shower. I am *not* in the mood. Hell, baby shower or not, I am angry at the world right about now. But I am especially angry at Kaylin. He keeps promising me that he's going to get Trae out, but I don't think he can pull it off. That's why I need a face-to-face. I cursed him out a couple of times for stringing me along, and today, I plan on cursing him out again. He hasn't even called me back. I know it's because he doesn't want to hear my mouth. But he's going to continue to hear it until my husband is back with his family.

Pulling into Angel's driveway, the valet grabs the door. They were still setting up. I had no idea she was going to do it this big. Large stuffed animals scattered on the grounds, servers pushing carts of hors d'oeuvres, the balloons have trinkets attached, and waiters carrying trays of champagne. The car was barely shut off when the boys took off running toward the backyard. I don't have the energy or will to chase after them. Not today.

My phone vibrated. Speak of the devil. It's him. "Kay, we need to talk."

"Aw, shit. I'm Kay? Not Kaylin? You mad at me again?"

"We need to talk. Where are you, Kay?" I wasn't in the mood to play with him.

"Red said you wasn't at the house yet. I was just checking on you. Where are you? It's your baby shower. Don't you think you should be there?"

I was sick and tired of Kaylin playing my warden. "I just pulled up. I'm here."

"Good, this will be good for you. You need to get out more."

"Kay, I swear, I am getting real impatient with you and all of your suggestions about what I need. What I need is for you get my husband out!" I don't know how much longer I can stand this. I've been praying day and night that Trae would be home before the baby gets here. "How much longer?" I felt my eyes welling up. "At least if I could have stayed in Cali, I would be closer to him. You said he would be home by—"

"Bye, Tasha."

And just like that, he was gone.

"No, this nigga didn't just hang up on me!" I stormed up the front steps and into the house.

"Surpriiiiiise!" everyone yelled out. Not sure why they were yelling surprise. This shower was no surprise. All you had to do was go onto Angel's Instagram page.

Kyra was the first to grab me and give me a big hug. Our bellies bumped. We were both big and fat. I stepped back to get a good look at her, and she was glowing. Jaz, Faheem, Bo, and Shanna gave me hugs. After I greeted everyone, I asked Angel where Kaylin was.

"He's not here yet. He's on his way. Why? What's the matter? You don't look too good. And where are the boys? You know Aisha is waiting for them," Angel said.

"They ran around back." I headed for the stairs.

"Where are you going, Tasha?"

"I'm not feeling well. I'm going to lie down, Angel."

"Tasha, don't even try it. I know you. Stay your ass down here. You need to be around your family. They traveled far to see you."

"Fuck family, Angel. That's how I'm feeling right about now. And I told you I don't feel well. Plus, my family is locked away in California somewhere. I don't know if he's dead or alive."

"Bitch, you know what? Nope. I'm not going to ruin my peace and this family atmosphere. Go, Tasha. Go and lock your angry ass in the bathroom, for all I care. I don't give a shit." She waved me off and walked away.

That's exactly what I was going to do. Lock my ass in a room somewhere. I wasn't feeling festive. I made it to what used to be my old room, slammed the door, fell across the bed, and started crying.

Faheem

All praise is due to Allah. I must constantly thank Him for getting me and my family out of Atlanta safe and sound. If I had stayed another day trying to avenge my son's death, I know they all would have been dead, even me, or worse, I would be facing life. I thank Allah for giving me the strength to let go and leave. It was the hardest thing I ever had to do.

So here we are back in Jersey. It feels strange. Almost as if I shouldn't be here. A feeling that I can't shake, that's telling me to not get too comfortable. I asked Allah to show me a sign. I just pray that I recognize it when it comes. But for now, I can only trust that His will is being done.

Allah gives life, and He takes it away. My son was in my life for less than a year before he was taken from me. Burying your child comes with a type of anguish that I can't describe. I keep asking why I had to even meet him. It was a fluke that I did. I mean, who meets their son for the first time by bumping into him at a mall? That alone was surreal. His mom, Oni, never told me she was pregnant. She just upped

18

and moved to Atlanta, and when we saw her, she had the nerve to try to run. What person in their right mind would do some shit like that?

With each passing day, I am feeling a little stronger, getting my mind back right. And it feels good to be back around family, simply chilling—no hustling, no drama, no guns. It feels even better to see Jaz smiling. I know it has been hard on her to see me hurting the way that I was. But my son's death made her and my bond that much tighter.

I may even get lucky by the baby shower rubbing off on her. Maybe she'll start feeling guilty and be ready to give me a son. Who knows?

Rick

Nothing like the Big Apple. I made a name for myself as a detective here. It would be nice to move out here. Start all over. LA was nothing but trouble. Arizona is too damn hot. I have to figure it all out. But for now, my main focus is for Nina and Kyra to get on board with my plans to love them both. I'm more concerned with breaking Nina and Kyra out of this Western civilization mind-set—all that brainwashing and negativity when it comes to the other woman. When a lady knows that she is that "other woman," or that "side chick," she willingly plays her position. She waits and sneaks around to be with, talk to, fuck, hang out . . . the relationship has to exist on the low, and she handles the shit with skill. Sometimes for years. So, what's the problem with a nigga placing all the cards on the table? Later for all of that sneaking

19

around bullshit. This is the new millennium. Men have multiple families these days. I didn't lie to either one of them. No need to sneak around. It takes too much time. It doesn't even have to be announced who I am with. As long as they know it's just the two of them, they should be happy with the situation. They both claim they are in love with me and want to be with me, so why can't we all just get along and coexist peacefully?

They both know my situation is unique, and I get it that it can be hard for a woman to accept something like this. I love two women. One who I thought was dead, and the other one who I fell in love with after the fact. What the fuck am I supposed to do? I didn't know that I could love two women at the same time.

I stepped into the house, and Kyra was talking animatedly with Jaz and Angel. When she turned around to see who they were looking at, it was too late. I was already grabbing her hand.

"Angel!" she yelled out. "You promised. You gave me your word."

"She promised you what, Kyra? That I wouldn't be here for *our* baby shower? That I wouldn't be here to celebrate this special occasion? You really need to stop the bullshit, Kyra." I pulled her toward what appeared to be the kitchen. "We need to talk, and I mean now."

"Rick, I told you to let me deal with this *my* way. I only asked that you respect my request."

"There isn't anything to deal with. The only thing you

need to do is work on the idea of all of us being one happy family."

"Go ahead with that bullshit. Kick rocks, nigga, and respect my space, Rick. I'm trying to wrap my head around the situation I'm in."

"Fine, Kyra. I'm on the verge of giving you all the fucking space you'll ever need. You know where to find me." I left her standing right there in the kitchen. I wasn't going to keep repeating myself. She was either going to get it or not. There was nothing else to discuss.

Chapter Two

Kaylin

H *ow did I become the designated driver when it's time to pick up the niggas just getting out of the bing?* As soon as that question left my mind, I got my answer. *Nigga, be thankful you doing the picking up, instead of somebody picking your ass up.* I'm straight, Lord. Say no more.

I glanced at the AP on my wrist and jumped out of Angel's GLE. I had to pick it up from the detail shop. Our daughter, Jahara, and her little buddies spilled Lord knows what all on the backseat and floor. Even though it was roomy and glided across the highway, it still screamed *girl* to me. I preferred much more power and style. The 600 was my steelo.

I got out and leaned against it, waiting on my partner in crime, Trae-muthafuckin'-Macklin. If this was a few years ago, I would have went all out for my nigga, but the team been through so many jail releases, that shit old.

After about ten minutes, I was getting impatient. "A'ight, nigga. You said 2:00. No text. No call. Whatup?" About fifteen minutes later, the plane hit the tarmac. It had to be a boss feeling to leave prison and jump onto your own private jet.

After about five minutes, the door came open, and the steps were rolled up to the side of the jet. Trae appeared with two suitcases and a backpack as he made it down the stairs. He set them on the dolly and raced back up. *Damn. How much luggage can he possibly have?* This time, he came back down with shopping bags. *What the fuck?* How this nigga had time to go shopping, I had no clue.

He looked over at me. "Yo! You gonna just stand there and look or help a nigga out?"

"Do I look like I'm wearing a baggage claim uniform? Dude got it. That's what you payin' him for." I pointed to the white dude carrying a box. "Just have him dump the shit on the dolly and roll the shit over. It doesn't take a rocket scientist to figure that out," I yelled out and popped the trunk, trying to hide my excitement.

"Yo, he better not dump my shit on the cart. Yo! Carry the shit over! I got breakables in them bags!" he yelled at the staffer. Then he turned to me and said, "Thanks for your words of wisdom. But, for real, my nigga, you know you glad to see me." He was all smiles as he made his way over to the ride pushing the luggage rack.

"No, I'm not, nigga!" I joked back as me and my brother from another mother slapped fives and hugged at the same time. I watched as he loaded up the trunk. I meant it when I said I didn't work for baggage claim.

"Lazy ass," he mumbled. "Tasha still don't know, right?"

"Nah, nigga, she doesn't know."

"Good. Let's roll."

Trae

Oh yeah! A nigga was finally home free, and I was feeling good. I was feeling like I was starting life over. Kay picked me up from the airport and was running his mouth, but I was tuning him out. My thoughts were on my wife and kids.

Excited, I opened the door before he could come to a full stop. "Damn, valet, nigga?"

"Angel, dawg. She misses her girls and wanted to go all out. Wait until you see the setup inside. She has chefs, carving stations set up. Crab cakes flown in from Maryland . . . all types of bullshit. She has turned the crib into a reality show."

I followed Kay up the stairs and stood behind him as he opened the door. Everyone got quiet because they all knew that I was coming and that I wanted to surprise Tasha. Of course, I was excited to see everybody. Plus, the fellas and I had some business to attend to, but I would catch up with them later. It was all understood as Angel motioned for me to go upstairs. She and Kay were right behind me. I knew what room she was in because the door was shut, and I could feel the negative vibes. Kaylin told me that she had turned into a real B.I.T.C.H. since she had been in New York. I had to laugh. That's my baby, and I know I hurt her, but one thing for sure, no matter what our bond was like, if she had to, she would wait on me if it was forever.

I turned the doorknob, but it was locked. I looked back at Angel who was fumbling with her camera, and then at Kay

24

who motioned for me to be quiet.

He banged on the door. "Tasha, open up this damn door! The party is downstairs, not up here in the room with you."

"Later for you, Kay! And if I was you, I would get the hell away from my door. I am *not* feeling you right now."

"*Your* door? This is *my* house."

"Kaylin, leave me alone, please."

"What did I do, Tasha?"

"What the fuck is really going on? Where is my husband, Kaylin? What aren't you telling me? Why do you feel that you have to hide shit from me?"

"Tasha, open the door. I told you I was working on it. These things take time." Kay was smiling as he was talking to her. Angel was trying to hold back her laughter. But from the base in Tasha's voice, I knew she was pissed.

"Just give me a little more time."

"Fuck that, Kay! Your time is up. I'm going back to my house in California this week, and you won't be able to stop me."

"Your ass ain't going nowhere until Trae says so. He asked me to keep an eye on his family, and I can't do that with you way across the country. So, your ass ain't going nowhere—even if you have to be here another year, or however long it takes."

That's when the door flew open, and my wife looked as if she was ready to draw blood. That's right when Angel said, "Surprise, bitch!" and kept clicking her camera. "I got your evil ass on camera. You feel stupid, don't you?"

"Babeeee." She covered her mouth as the tears welled up in her eyes.

"Now what? Say it, Tasha! Tell me I'm the man," Kaylin boasted while pounding on his chest. "Go ahead! Tell me! Say it!"

"Nigga, leave my wife alone," I told him as I grabbed her and hugged her tight. "Daddy's home now." I backed my wife into the bedroom and kicked the door shut. Everyone burst out laughing.

Tasha

Oh my God. This wasn't happening. The room was spinning, but my heart and head were no longer heavy. I couldn't believe it. My baby is home! He's finally home. *Whoop! Whoop! Whoop!* My baby's home! That's how I'm feeling right now. A few minutes ago, I was one angry, miserable—did I say angry—bitch. I could no longer hold it in. The Almighty is always right on time. I was right at the edge, and He sent me an angel. My angel. Ooh, I am *so* happy.

"Daddy's home now."

I melted into his arms as he kicked the door shut and held me tight. At that moment, even though I knew everything was going to be okay, I really broke down and cried like a baby. He patiently rubbed my back and kissed my ear. "I'm here now."

When I finally got ahold of myself, he stepped back and looked me over from head to toe. He smiled. "Your ass is fat." I burst out crying once again. "But I like it. I like it a

26

lot."

I rushed back into his arms. Now I was safe. I had my man home. The only man I wasn't afraid to love. Words could not do justice to how I was feeling.

He grabbed both of my cheeks and kissed me softly on the lips. "Bae, stop crying. You trying to make me sad?" I held him tighter. We just stood in the middle of the floor enjoying the moment. The moment where no words were needed to be spoken. This was our moment, and I didn't want it to end. I was elated. Relieved. Happy. Thankful. You name it.

"You gonna tell daddy all about it, or are you going to just keep crying? Get it out. What's on your mind?"

His hands slid down and were now caressing my ass cheeks.

"Don't do that, Trae. You are making me feel so fat."

"I told you I like it."

"Well, I don't. I'm fat. Miserable. I hate New York. The kids are driving me crazy. They miss their dad. Kaylin kept lying to me. You stopped calling and writing. It was looking as if I was going to be going through this pregnancy all by myself. I'm seven months, Trae. Having another baby, while taking care of the three we have by myself was stressing me out. Everything was coming to a boiling point, Trae."

"Damn. Is there anything else?" he teased.

"Whatever, Trae. You know it's not everything. But hell, my baby is home now, and I feel my swagswayzee coming back already."

"Oh, so your man bringing your swag and your sway

back?"

"My swag and my sway."

"Swagswayzee." I was actually smiling.

"Well, good. Now wipe the snot off your face. You got my shirt all messed up."

"Whatever." I kissed him on the lips, snot and all. Then I wobbled to the bathroom to get myself together. I loved this man so much.

When I came out of the bathroom, Trae got right to the point, as usual. "We both are going to need your swag and your sway to get us back right. You feel me?" The elephant in the room needed to be acknowledged, and Trae wasted no time doing so. Eight or nine months ago, our marriage was unraveling quicker than niggas lining up to cop, and then the po po rolls up. It was all because of him fucking with some Asian bitch, Charli Li. I hate saying the bitch's name. And I retaliated by fucking the next nigga, Kyron Santos. I hate saying his name just as much.

Trae

Tasha and I still had the Kyron issue to address. Shit had moved so fast, and it was never the right time to have "the talk."

"You know we got some shit to address, right? And we gonna have to arm ourselves against the shit that's going to be coming at us from everywhere."

Tasha pushed me away from her. "As long as you don't try to blame everything on me, I'm good. Because, keeping it

28

real, *you* started this shit. I just set it off and finished it."

"But, Tasha, you didn't have to fuck the nigga and get into a relationship."

"Trae. Oh my God. Baby, do you *hear* what you're saying? You're conveniently leaving out how you fucked a bitch and got *her* pregnant. Which would likely have been a *relationship* if I hadn't tripped the bitch, made her fall down the stairs and abort that bastard. And—"

"Oh, so the truth comes out now. You did trip her."

"Nigga, you know I did but don't try to change the subject. We can't forget how you fucked yet *another* bitch and gave me trichomoniasis, nigga. You better be glad I'm still here."

"What's that supposed to mean?" I wanted to know.

"Take it how you want to, Trae. You know what the fuck I mean!"

"No, I don't. Tell me."

"Trae, you haven't been home for a full twenty minutes, and we are fighting already. What? What are we going to do? Let's get the shit out now."

I knew I should have waited to bring that up. I had planned to do just that. Now I had to diffuse the situation or mess up my homecoming and all of the trouble we went to pull this day off. "What we always do. Get through it. Wade through all of the bullshit. Fight to keep us. Fight to keep what we've built. Is it worth it to you? It's worth it to me."

"Yes, we are worth it. You know that. But I don't want to fight today. I'm beat down, baby. Can I enjoy my husband for a couple of days, please? If you want me or need me to

29

still be that ride or die, I will do that. Just let me know if that's what we are doing. I was angry at you. You were angry at me. We're even. So, tell me, Trae. Right here. Right now. *What are we going to do?*"

"We'll start by taking it one day at a time." I began rubbing my baby's stomach.

"I want to enjoy this moment," Tasha told me again. I wanted to enjoy it too. Tasha and my kids were my everything. "You are home, baby. And I'm still in love with you."

That was soothing music to my ears, like an old Mary J. Blige song. Tasha moved close to me and kissed me on the lips. The kiss turned my dick from angry to happy. Now my problem was to control myself until we got home.

Tasha

Trae and I were still standing in the middle of the floor hugging and talking when we heard the various knocks on the door.

"Uh-oh, daddy, I think you have some little, anxious visitors. Somebody spilled the beans that their dad was in the house."

"Hey, Ma! Mommy!" The knocks were coming harder and faster.

Trae kissed me on the lips once again. "I love you," I told him, not wanting to turn my baby loose.

"Love you more. Let me see my little troops." His eyes lit up.

30

Even though he always tells me, "Tasha, you are my everything," I beg to differ. I think those boys are his everything. "Okay, but you gotta let me capture this moment." I got my phone ready, and then motioned for Trae to stand to the side. I pressed record and opened the door halfway. "Guys, Mommy was trying to get some rest. What's up?"

Caliph, our youngest, tried to squeeze past me. "Ma, Aisha said my daddy was here."

"Is my dad here?" Kareem, one of the twins, asked.

"My daddy is here!" Shaheem, the other twin responded.

"My dad is not here. Just Mommy." Caliph chimed in, obviously disappointed.

I stepped back, and Trae appeared. They all yelled and bum-rushed him at the same time.

Priceless.

Kyra

What a baby shower! I thought to myself. Angel outdid herself. Valet. Chefs. Servers. Scrumptious food. She obviously has too much time on her hands. She had the four of us together for old times' sake. And I really appreciated that. And everyone had their man. Even me if only for a moment. I was so happy to see Trae, because Tasha had us all worried. I don't think she could have made it another day without him. Every time I looked over at them, she was holding onto him for dear life.

On the other hand, when I turned around and saw Rick, all

I could think about was smacking the shit out of Angel. We had several conversations about not inviting him. I explained to her that I was not ready to deal with him. I am not going to forgive her for this one.

We were standing on the back porch trying to talk quietly. "Kyra, the man wanted to come and be a part of your baby shower. You are carrying his baby, for crying out loud."

"You promised me, Angel. I asked—no—*begged*, that you let me deal with this *my* way. He's not leaving that bitch, Angel. You know what that's telling me?" I couldn't hold back the tears.

"Kyra, he's telling her that he's not leaving you. Shit, she feels the same way! Both of y'all are pregnant, and he is making it clear that he will continue to see her and continue to see you. And the way I see it, do what you gotta do but don't let her have him. Don't lie down on that shit. One of y'all is going to get sick of it, so let it be her. You said you deserve to be happy. Just say the word and I will help you get him. I know it's a fucked-up situation, but it's not his fault. And it's not her fault. We all thought you were gone, Kyra. None of us knew. He tried to move on. We tried to move on. But you came back into all of our lives, thank God. You need to check yourself and try to deal with this a little better than what you're doing."

"Oh, please, Angel. Tell me this. How would *you* deal with this? What would *you* do?"

"I hope deal with it a little better than how you are. Try my best not to be too judgmental. Kyra, listen. The man loves you. You love him. Try to work it out. Do it for the baby. I think it's divine to be pregnant and in love and with your love. That's all I can say." She turned and walked away.

I was left standing on the back porch, watching the kids run around, carefree, having the time of their lives. Rick eased up behind me and placed both hands gently on my belly. "I miss you." He kissed me on the cheek, and then on my neck. I closed my eyes. "I'm not going anywhere, Kyra. Just wanted to make sure that you understood that."

"So, again, let me make sure I understand. You want me, you, and her to be one happy family?" I removed his hands from around my belly and was now pacing back and forth.

"Ma, can I go spend the night with the twins and Auntie Tasha?" Aisha ran up on the back porch. Kareem was right behind her. They both were dripping wet from the pool.

"No, Aisha! My mom already told you not tonight because my dad is home." Kareem ratted her out.

"Aisha and Kareem, go back and play. I'm talking to Rick."

"Kyra, stop twisting this around to be so negative. It don't have to be negative."

"Listen to yourself, Rick. Your line of thinking is making me dizzy. I gotta lie down." I was feeling light-headed, and I had to go and lean up against the wall. I closed my eyes.

I felt Rick next to me. "Kyra, are you all right?" He grabbed my hand.

"I'm fine. I need to lie down. I tried to tell you I wasn't ready to have this conversation." I made my way to the stairs, and, of course, Rick was right behind me. I went straight for the bed.

Mari

I sent Kay a text to come outside. The package I was holding onto was burning my hands. I had to see Kay. Plus, I needed to ask him if I was the only one mourning his brother Kyron's death. After the funeral, the only person who consistently kept in touch was Kendrick. He seemed more distraught than Kay was. Was I the *only* person seeking closure?

With that on my mind and the package in my hands, I ended up in front of the home of Kay and Angel Santos. Cars were parked in the driveway and in front of the house. I saw the baby shower balloons and realized that now wasn't a good time, obviously, but I had to pee. I double-parked, grabbed the envelope, and got out of the car.

Kaylin was coming out of the front door. *Damn.* He resembled Kyron so much, especially when he smiled.

"Hey, baby sis. What's good? How are you?" He gave me hug.

"Right now, I need to use your restroom. Do you mind? And then I have a package that I want to pass on. But I want to talk to you about it first. I need to use your bathroom."

"Come on in. We're just having a little get-together."

"A little get-together? It hardly looks little."

"It's all good." He held the front door open for me and waved me into the house. Whoever were the recipients of this shower would not have to buy their baby anything for a real long time. "Red, look who stopped by," he said.

She turned around surprised. "Mari?" Angel rushed over and gave me a hug. "What brings you all the way on this side of town? Is everything okay?" Angel asked. I could see her surprise turn to concern.

"I'm okay. I needed to get something to Kay, and I figured since I was in the area, I might as well stop by. When I saw all of the cars, I said I would come back another time, but my bladder had other ideas."

"Oh, my bad. Go ahead. I know you remember where the bathroom is."

Angel guided me to the bathroom, not introducing me to anyone. I caught a few glances. I closed the door and rushed to do what I came inside to do. But I still saw her. I saw them. Or were my eyes playing tricks on me? Tasha and Trae were sitting on the sofa all cuddled up. He was whispering in her ear. She was smiling and glowing. I thought he was in Cali in jail. And she's pregnant. Who is she pregnant by?

I washed and dried my hands and grabbed the package. I stepped out of the bathroom and needed to make sure my eyes weren't playing tricks on me.

There she was. Glowing. Happy. All cozy up under her man. The more I watched their exchange, the more I saw how she looked at him, how he looked at her, whispering in her ear, her lips curled into a permanent smile. She has it all. Why the fuck did she need Kyron? Her happy ass was the cause of all the damn drama from the day Kyron stepped foot out of that prison. I made my way back into the bathroom.

Chapter Three

Angel

L *ord have mercy!* I called myself planning the perfect baby shower. And like I mentioned before, the only drama I anticipated was with Rick and Kyra. And I was good with that. But Mari? She threw me a curveball. I watched as she came out of the bathroom, headed in the direction of Tasha and Trae. She held out a big envelope, exchanged words with Trae before he took it, and then she rushed back into the bathroom. *What the fuck?* I banged on the door and made her open it. Now we were huddled in the bathroom, and she was crying as I tried to calm her down, passing her Kleenex after Kleenex. The box was now damn near empty.

"Angel, you don't have to lie. I understand that she's your girl and everything. But you don't have to lie."

"Mari, of course she's my girl. She's like my sister. But do the math. Kyron passed how long ago? Yes, it's close, but not close enough. Plus, she had a DNA test done. So, chill. It's not his baby!" I handed her the last of the Kleenex. Where the fuck is her head? I got the impression that she didn't believe me.

"I'm sorry. Please accept my apology." She released a deep sigh. "The more time that passes since his death, the more depressed I get. I can't seem to shake him. And plus, it just feels like I'm the only one who wants to know what happened to him. And why? Does anyone else even care, Angel? Believe me when I say I'm trying to let it go, but I can't. No matter how hard I try. I'm really trying. It's probably why I ended up here, because I can't let it go!"

"Mari, keep it real. This is me you're talking to. You ending up here has every damn thing to do with that envelope, doesn't it? What's in it? Why did you give it to Trae? You didn't know he was going to be here. I mean, what the fuck!"

She rolled her eyes at me. "The sessions, Angel."

"What do you mean sessions?"

"Recorded sessions of Kyron. He didn't know that I arranged for him to have a sit-down with the psychologist. I wanted to get to the bottom of what was driving him to be with her. What wasn't I doing?"

"So, if you wanted to know what was going on with Tasha and Kyron, why are you giving that envelope to Trae? That's some dirty shit, Mari."

"Of course you would say that. Tasha is your girl. But I want him to know what I know about my man. Tasha is his wife. I know everything. They were in love, Angel, and Trae has the right to know. I think he deserves to know the depth of their relationship."

What doctor will release private recorded sessions of their patients? That had to be a state institutional doctor. Nothing to lose. Just like Mari. This bitch had to be delusional. In love? Bullshit! Kyron was pussy drunk, and he fell right into Tasha's web. She got revenge while getting dicked down, while at the same time, she still got her man. I'm sure there won't be a repeat performance. Nevertheless, she got that off. But now, Mari is telling me that she gave Trae some tapes that would more than likely unravel their marriage ties for good this time. I foresee more harm than good in that envelope. I needed to get it from him. I raced out of the bathroom leaving her messy ass in there.

"Trae, let me talk to you for a minute." I'm looking for the envelope, but I don't see it. "Trae!" I grabbed his arm, but he wouldn't budge. I stood over him and Tasha. "I need to talk to you for a minute. And bring the envelope that Mari just gave you."

He simply looked at me, not responding, and he still wouldn't get up off the couch. Tasha was nestled under him, her arm snaked around his, unwilling to let him go. But I didn't give up.

"Trae, where is that envelope? Let me get that from you right quick."

"And why would I do that?" he asked me.

I stood tall, hands on my hips looking down at him and his wife. "You know this is some bullshit, and y'all don't need this, Trae."

"Don't worry about it, Angel. I appreciate you looking out, but it's all good," he said.

I looked at a stone-faced Tasha, and then back at Trae. He was too damn calm for me and obviously high off of weed, being home and being back with his family, or something. And Tasha was obviously down with wherever he was going

39

with regarding this charade. "All right then. Suit yourself. I'm going to mind my own business." I was forced to let it go. But they can't say that I didn't try. As if on cue, Mari came rushing by, heading for the front door. I turned and followed behind her.

"Are you going to be okay?" I asked, not allowing her to leave before I had my say.

"I'll be fine, Angel."

"Okay, cool. But, Mari, I want you keep in touch. You know you are like family, and because of that, I know you won't mind me saying that you shouldn't have given that envelope to anyone. Not Kaylin. Not Trae. Not Tasha. It is now the past. Kyron is gone, and you need to move on. What's done is done."

"It's not done, Angel. That's where *you're* wrong." With that said, she left the house, and then she looked back at me and said, "You're right; Kyron is gone, and he's not coming back. But I'm not done. I will *never* be done." She didn't look back as she headed down the street and jumped into her truck.

Damn it! I had to admit that I just allowed her to fuck up my awesome mood. I paced back and forth trying to get myself together. I was today's hostess with the mostess, I kept repeating to myself. That was . . . up until this point. Overall, I felt as if I was controlling everyone's good mood, but now that my mood was fucked up, everyone else's was getting ready to be fucked up as well.

"Yo, what's up, Auntie? What up! What up! What up!"

Instantly, a smile formed across my lips. Forget about

Mari for now. Kevin was here, Tasha's baby brother! And since I considered her my sister, he was my little nephew. He was coming up the street with a young lady rocking the coldest Giuseppes I'd seen in a while. I just wasn't shelling out $2,200 for them. And she was carrying a little boy who looked to be around two years old. I made it down the steps and met him at the driveway and gave him a big hug. "Glad you made it. I didn't tell your sister because I wanted to surprise her. You know she's going to be so glad to see you."

"She just ought to be! Her ass been in New York all this time and didn't even call me or tell me that she was here."

"Don't be mad at her. She doesn't want to be here, and she has this big chip on her shoulder, a big-ass belly, and a whole bunch of drama going on, as usual." He started laughing. I then directed my attention to the young lady that he was with.

"My bad, Auntie. Let me introduce you to my bae. Auntie, this is my bae. Bae, meet my auntie."

Right on cue, the little boy started throwing up. "Oh, Carlos!" she said. The three of us stood there watching the baby hurl.

"Good. His fever should break now," Kevin said, leaning down and wiping the child's mouth. Carlos was standing there head back, eyes closed, screaming at the top of his little lungs.

His mother swooped him up. "I need to get him cleaned up."

"Of course. Follow me." I couldn't wait to question her about the baby. "Does he need some juice or Tylenol or anything? As you will see, we are shy of a football team around here today. Whatever you need for this little cutie let me know."

"Bae, take care of my li'l man. Yo! Is that Faheem?" Kevin asked. "Bae, I'll be in there." He kissed her on the cheek and went to see Faheem.

Tasha

Finally, I was in a baby shower mood, now that my bae was by my side. I was even excited to look at all of the gifts and to enjoy the atmosphere that a couple of hours ago, I wasn't a part of. Trae leaned over and whispered into my ear, "Yo, beautiful, I hope you're ready."

"Ready for what?"

"Tonight."

"Tonight?"

"You heard me. We fucking *all* night. And I mean *all* night," he emphasized.

I giggled as I kissed him gently on the lips and felt myself getting moist. "I hope *you* are ready."

"Oh yeah? It's going down like that?"

"You *know* it is." I was getting more excited by the second.

"Bring it on then. I just don't want to hear you crying out, 'Oh, please, Trae, please, I can't come anymore; pleeeese stop.'"

"Whatever." I couldn't help but close my eyes and visualize it. I would have to prepare myself mentally because

Trae . . . well, let's just say I knew it was coming. Trae will make good on his promise. I could beg and plead all I wanted, but when he got in that zone . . . He was in the zone. All I could do was ride the roller coaster. I was enjoying the visual. But when I opened my eyes, it felt as if I was in a bad dream. "Who-what-is that Mari? I know damn well Angel did *not* invite her to my baby shower."

"Apparently, she did," Trae said. "And she's coming right this way."

"I swear, Trae, I am not up for any—"

"Chill out." He squeezed my hand.

Mari stood over the two of us. "Hello, Trae. I wasn't expecting to see you here. I stopped by to see Kay and to ask him to make sure that you receive this. But since you're here, I can put it in your hands myself." She was holding a large brown envelope.

"What's inside?" Trae looked at the envelope as if she were carrying a ticking time bomb.

"Some recorded sessions that I think you need to hear. Take them please. I have copies."

Kaylin stepped over and tried to grab the envelope, but Trae placed it behind his back. "No, I'm good, dawg. She said it's just some tapes that I needed to listen to. And I want to know what's on these tapes so we're going to check them out."

The look on Kaylin's face let me know that he was going to get into Mari's ass. "Let me holla at you, Mari," he told her, grabbing her by the arm.

What the fuck? I looked at the envelope, and I could say that now my mood was beginning to sink.

Fast.

"Yo, didn't I just say it?" I barely got the words out of my mouth. Trae reached back and held up the envelope. "I told you shit was going to be coming out of nowhere. Life comes full circle for you, and the things you thought you got away with come right back to bite you in the ass. But again, I told you we gonna handle shit together. Ride or die. Our shit is unbreakable. You feel me?"

"I'm unbreakable," I mumbled.

"I can't hear you."

"Unbreakable," I said louder while wondering what bullshit was going to brew up from him listening to the tapes. I felt my mood slowly sinking right back down to where it was when I came to the shower.

Rick

After I fluffed up Kyra's pillows, I went to get a bottle of water and a warm cloth. Seeing her small body curled up into a knot on the bed had me worried.

"Kyra, maybe we should call an ambulance."

"Rick, I'm not in labor, and I'm not dying. I'm just a little light-headed." She unraveled and sat up. I opened the water and placed the bottle to her lips. She took a few swallows, bumping off half the bottle.

"I hope you're not dehydrated," I told her as she lay back onto the headboard.

"I'm fine." She closed her eyes, and I placed the damp cloth to her forehead.

"Kyra, I—"

"Please. Not—*ohhhhhh*," She grabbed her stomach.

"What? What is it, Kyra?" I was trying to remain calm.

"It felt like she just did two backward flips."

"How do you know it's a girl?"

"The doctor told me."

"When were you planning on telling me, the daddy, that I have a baby girl on the way?"

She didn't say anything.

"Kyra, you know you on some straight bullshit, right?"

She slid her blouse up, and I saw some lumps travel across her stomach. My baby girl was amped. "There's a little too much drama for you out here, Destiny, isn't it? Is that what you're trying to tell us?" I leaned over and placed a few kisses across her belly.

"Destiny? I'm not naming her Destiny!"

Kyra removed the cloth from her forehead and was now staring at me wide-eyed.

"Baby, the sooner you figure out I AM DADDY and that means your DADDY and the baby that you are carrying's DADDY, the easier shit will be for you. And like I said, I'm naming my daughter Kyra Destiny." I went back to gently kissing her belly.

Rick

Kyra Destiny. I liked the way that sounded. "Hey, baby,

this is your father. Your daddy loves you," I told my unborn baby girl.

"I'm serious, Rick, that is not going to be my baby girl's name."

"She's not *your* baby, Kyra. She's *our* baby."

"She's *my* baby, not *our* baby. I wanted you. I wanted it to be me and you."

"It *is* me and you, dammit, Kyra!" The tone and no-nonsense in my voice must have startled the shit out of her. She began to tremble as the tears rolled down her cheeks.

"Rick, I've made up my mind. I can't, and I won't."

"Kyra, you haven't even tried so stop this bullshit right now! It ends right here, right now, *this* moment. You are *my* woman. We are going to be together, as a family, and be fucking happy about it."

Chapter Four

Kevin

"Yo, Fah!" He and Bo were standing there facing the kids, watching them play. I was cool with Bo, but Faheem was that nigga, my nigga. Coming up, Jaz and my sister Roz, y'all call her Tasha, were the closest of the four girls. Of course, they would hang out a lot, and I knew Faheem from being Jaz's boyfriend. He would school me about the dope game. I had nothing but respect for him. On top of that, he was one of the homies from Trenton, New Jersey.

"Kev, I thought that was you. What up, soldier?"

"You know what it is. Just came by to check on my sister." As we dapped each other up I turned to Bo. "What up, man?"

"You got it. Good to see you." We dapped up as well. Then I ducked and the ball hit Bo in the chest. "Yo, you got to stay on your toes!" We all started laughing, and he went after the ball and headed for the backyard.

"Fah, how long are you in town for?"

"Nigga, you ain't get the memo? I'm on the East Coast for good. Just waiting on Jaz to settle her school stuff. That's where we'll be settling down."

"Settling down? Oh, I forgot, you on triple G status!"

Faheem smiled that humble smile. "I wouldn't call it that.

47

I'm just chilling. What's good with you? I see you doing the family thing."

"Nah, nah. Not yet. That's shorty's son. I'm just helping out. Trying to get in where I fit in. I work for food," I joked.

"Yeah, right. I know you think you got nine lives. But you done used up how many already?"

"I used up about six or seven of them mufuckas, but c'mon, Unc, what else I'ma do? My parents were hustlers, my sisters were hustlers, Tasha married a hustler, my homies are hustlers. What else I'ma do? Get a 9 to 5? Four, five hunned a week? I'm not built like that. But, yo, trust me when I say it, I have a smooth situation; everything is behind the scenes."

"Just so you know, moving behind the scenes don't make you bulletproof or indictment proof. And who is she? Who *she* work for?"

"Her name is Lolita. She's a businesswoman. She has a bail bonds agency, and she runs the Jersey Flea Market. If you ever need anything, I got you. You looked out for me when it counted. I can't forget that."

"Kevin! Kevin! Come here, boy!" My sister was calling me as she walked, more like wobbled, down the street.

"Unc, I'ma get back with you," I told Faheem.

"Yeah, 'cause she look like she about to whip that ass!"

"Whatever, yo!" I said before turning my attention to my sister. "Damn, sis, you stay pregnant! What number is this . . . nine?"

"Damn right," she said, right before she smacked me

upside my head.

"Look who's talking! Why didn't you tell me you had a son? What is *wrong* with you?"

"Slow your roll, sis. He ain't mines. I'm just raising him for now." My sister glared at me as if she didn't believe me. "Why would I lie? If he was mines, I would tell you. He don't even look like me."

"Yes, he does, Kevin."

"Association breeds similarity, sis."

"Yeah, right!" She gave me a big hug. "There's something you're not telling me."

"Just like you didn't tell me you was no longer in Cali. What up with that?" I went to smack her upside her head; she ducked, but not before punching me in the chest.

Kaylin

Bo, Trac, and I were in the basement getting our smoke on and shooting a little pool. I couldn't help but think that anytime Red is doing anything with the girls, there's bound to be some drama. Which reminded me, I haven't seen Kyra or Rick in a while. Which meant that I needed to check on things and make sure things are going well.

"I'll be back in a few." I went upstairs to check the guest rooms. I tapped on the first door. "Kyra? Rick? Y'all good?"

The door flew open and immediately slammed shut. It flew open again and Rick said, "We good!"

"I hope so. You sure about that?"

"Trust and believe before we come out of this room, we

are going to be one big-ass happy family." And he slammed the door again.

I checked the other rooms. Everything was good. My daughter Jahara's bedroom looked as if a tornado went through it. Being an only child, in this house, whenever she gets some company, just like her mom and dad, she plays the ultimate hostess. But Jahara pulls out every doll, video game, and just plain junk. Just because.

I went downstairs to check on my wife. When she looked up and saw me, she said, "Kaylin, speak to your daughter."

"Jay, behave please, ma'am."

"Dad, I am."

"She is not. She's being rude. Any other day she wants to play with Derek and Ashley. Now, she wants to act all new. I'm not allowing them to come over anymore."

"Jay, we spoke about this before, didn't we?"

"I know, Dad. But you said I didn't have to play with them when I didn't want to. And today, I don't want to because I have enough kids to watch."

Angel looked at me and rolled her eyes. "I need to be in the loop on some of these conversations, Kaylin. Go back outside, Jahara. And treat people how you want to be treated," she snapped.

"Yes, ma'am."

I grabbed Angel's hand, but she tried to snatch it away from me.

"What?"

"Don't what me, Kaylin."

"Come here, baby. Dance with me."

"You can't be going behind my back, Kaylin. You're not around when she's begging their parents to let them come play with her."

I tried not to laugh. "Red, it's no big deal. Her family is over. She doesn't need them today."

"Kaylin!"

"Come here, baby." I embraced her. "Can your husband have this dance?" Ro James was asking for permission. "I just want to spend a little time with you," I sang into her ear as she tried to squirm away. But she couldn't. She eventually decided to relax and melt into my arms. I massaged her back and pressed up against her, waiting on permission and wanting that green light.

"Awwww, how sweet," Jaz teased as she walked by us, licking an ice-cream pop.

"So what's up? You givin' me that green light or what?"

"Tonight. I'ma allow you to do whatever you want to do to me."

"Whatever?"

"Whatever."

We swayed back and forth, both of us reveling in the moment.

"It's a blessing and a curse that I know you so well, Kaylin. Your dick is hard, but your mind is elsewhere. What's up?"

"Who is the chick over there in the corner?"

"She came with Kev. Why?"

51

"What's her name?"

"She introduced herself as Lolita."

"Lolita, huh?"

"Why? Do you know her?"

I kissed her on the forehead. "Thank you for the dance, baby."

"Where are you going, Kaylin?"

"Nowhere." I left her standing there.

"Trae, I need to holla at you. Meet me in the dining room." I went and found Bo and told him the same thing. I closed the double doors, but before I could turn around, Faheem was knocking and barging his way through.

"So this is where the party moved to."

"Yo. Check this out. Trae, look out there and tell me who that chick is."

Trae got up, cracked the doors, and closed them back. "I don't know. Who? Am I supposed to know her?"

"Yo, Trae, look again. Who does she resemble?"

Trae went back to the doors and cracked them again. This time I stood behind him. "Look at those eyes. Now look at how her mouth is shaped, yo. Yo, this shit is spooky. We got us a problem." Now, both Bo and Faheem were trying to get a peek.

"You know what? She look a little like Don Carlos." Trae finally caught on.

"Yo, I was starting to think you was getting slow. Yeah, but exactly."

Trae slid the doors shut. His jaws clenched. "What? He

spying on us now? Did we do something to have our loyalty questioned?"

"Who is she?" Bo asked.

Faheem

"Can someone explain to me what the fuck is going on? I thought we were having a celebration. Y'all Negroes done turned the party dark. I mean, this is supposed to be a joyous occasion, a family gathering, not the Situation Room." I was dead serious. The tension had gone from 0 to 60 in a matter of seconds.

"Can y'all excuse me and Trae for a few minutes?" Kay had the nerve to ask us.

"What?" Bo asked.

"Hold up. Hold up. How you going to insult me like that?" I couldn't believe that Kay asked us to leave the room.

"Yo, you took the words right out of my mouth. At least grant a nigga the respect and let me know what the situation is and give me the chance to say I'm in or not," Bo snapped.

"My brothers, y'all know that I meant no disrespect. As a matter fact, it's because of my respect for you that I'm asking y'all to leave the room. Everyone is at a point in their lives where they don't need any unnecessary drama or shit. We get that with our wives. But why would I get y'all involved in something that could disrupt everything? Where the outcome could be a toe tag or a jail cell?" Kaylin told us.

I wasn't trying to hear that shit. He and Trae knew that Bo and I were always down for whatever, especially when it came to the fam.

Trae was standing in the corner, head down, hands buried in his pocket. I needed to know what the hell was brewing.

"Trae, what's up?" That was Kaylin pretty much wanting to know from Trae if he wanted to involve us or not.

"Who did Kevin say that chick was?" Trae had turned his attention on me. I didn't know he knew that I had a conversation with Kevin.

"He said Lolita, but her street name is Seven."

"Seven!" Kaylin repeated. "Trae, I told you that was her."

"Her who?" I asked.

"Look, we might as well fill y'all in. Y'all gonna find out eventually anyway. Don Carlos's youngest daughter is named Seven. His seventh child. Right before I relocated to Cali, there was a number placed on her head."

"Don Carlos put a price on his own daughter's head?" Bo asked.

"Yeah, he did. Don't know why, but he did. You know how it is with family," Kay added.

Yeah, I know you know. Kyron is a good example of that. You know shit is serious when you have to take out your own flesh and blood.

"Oh, and now she just happens to show up here with a family member of ours? Fuck outta here. She not here by coincidence," Trae snapped.

"I don't know. It's possible that it could be a coincidence. But what are the odds? I think it's a test," Trae suggested.

"Okay, so do we call him and tell him she's here or what?"

Kaylin wanted to know.

Trae was staring at the girl. "Yeah, we need to do that. But first we need to be one hunned that it's her."

"Oh, it's her. I know it is." Kaylin pulled out his phone and snapped a picture of her. Then he was speaking into his phone.

Are you still looking for her?

And he sent the message with the photo attached. Then he said, "If he doesn't call us, it's nothing. If he does, we'll deal with it then.

"But in the meantime, I think we should pull Kevin's punk ass in here. I've always had my doubts about him. If he set us up, I'ma handle him personally." Trae was agitated, and it was obvious. After all, the man hasn't been out of jail for more than forty-eight hours, and now he's faced with *this?*

"If he's setting y'all up, who is he setting y'all up for? The girl or her father?" I was trying to figure it out.

"That's a good question. I don't see Don Carlos doing this, Trae. Think about it. He knows that if he needs something, all he has to do is say the word," Kay said. "Why all the underhanded spy shit?"

"I wish I knew the answer to that one," Trae said.

"Let me go grab his little ass. I'll have some fun with him. Gotta keep my skills sharp. Nothing personal. However, y'all know any nigga can get it. You can't have no attachments. You carryin', right?" I asked. Bo was, and, of course, he was. "Just follow my lead." He pulled out his piece and handed it to me. "Y'all meet me in the basement."

55

I found Kevin in the backyard, happily playing with the twins and the little boy that he said was not his. "Yo, Kev!"

He looked up, and I motioned toward the house. He swooped the baby up and came into the house. "What up, Unc?"

"The fellows are in the basement, about to get to blowing some trees."

"A'ight. A'ight. Let me get little man to his moms, and I'll be right there!"

Tasha

"Oh my. The dead has risen," I mumbled to Jaz as Rick and Kyra walked into the living room.

"Me and Rick are going for a ride. I'ma take Aisha with me," she told Angel.

"Kyra, you know them kids are out there enjoying themselves. Let her stay here," Angel said.

"If you want to take somebody, take the boys," I joked.

"Yeah, right. I hope you got that cleared with Mr. Macklin," Kyra remarked.

"I'm joking. I'm joking," I said. "But let her stay."

"We'll be right back." Kyra and Rick walked out the front door.

Kyra and I looked at each other but couldn't say what we really wanted to say because we had company. "What did you say your name was again?" I asked the chick who came in with my brother. For the most part, she was in and out of the house or on her phone. My brother introduced her as Lolita, but I heard her say something else when she was on the phone.

"I'm Lolita."

"Lolita, allow me to properly introduce myself. I'm Tasha, Kevin's sister. Pleased to meet you and little Carlos. He's soooo cute."

"Your brother carries a picture of you in his wallet. I feel like I already know you. He says that you are like his mother and his father."

I smiled. "Yes, we have a unique history. So, how long have y'all been together?" I wasn't letting her off that easy.

Lolita smiled. "How should I put this? Ummm, me and Kev have an understanding. It's more of very close business relationship."

"Soooo, you are saying that y'all are not a couple?"

"No. It's more of a casual, but close, business relationship."

"The baby? He looks like Kevin."

"Trust me. It's all business."

Faheem

"Yo, that dro smells good. I see I'm in the right place," Kevin said as he raced down the stairs.

As soon as he hit the bottom landing, I grabbed him, put him in a choke hold, and pressed the gun barrel against his temple. "Who sent you here?" I caught him by surprise.

"What? Why—why the fuck are you choking me? What? What I do? Trae? Trae!"

"Trae, can't help you. Who sent you here? Answer me, nigga!"

"No one. What do you mean? Angel called me! She said come see my sister."

I could smell the fear. I cocked back the barrel. "Don't make me get blood all over my shirt. My daughter gave me this for Father's Day," I threatened.

"Trae!" he yelled out.

"I suggest you answer the man. Because look over there. He already got the carpet rolled and ready to take your body away," Trae told him.

"I swear! Nobody sent me. C'mon, Fa!"

"Then who's the girl?"

"Lolita, man. Her name is Lolita."

"What's her *real* name? Her government name. You shackin' up with the chick, so don't tell me you don't know her personal shit. You ain't stupid."

"Lolita Sieta Calderon, man. C'mon, Unc! Why the fuck you have to hold a burner to my head, yo? You know me. I put in work for you! What's this about?" He had broken into a sweat.

"Let him go, Faheem," Kaylin told me.

I removed the barrel, and then pushed him hard, sending him crashing toward the rugs he thought were to wrap up his dead body. Bo helped him up and forced him into a chair.

"Angel invited me. What's this about?" His eyes were wide with shock.

I still have it.

58

"Did she tell you to bring her here today?" Kay asked.

"Naw, man. I told you, I'm here because Angel told me to come."

"Who does she work for?"

"Who does who work for? What do you mean?"

I placed my arms around his neck and squeezed. "You know what the fuck we mean.

Who does she work for? What's her front?"

He was gasping for air as I eased my choke hold. "She works for herself. She has a bail bonds agency. I don't know her dope connect. I just know that she runs both the East and South sides of Trenton."

"She runs with who, nigga? You? If you want to live, I suggest you stop being so vague,"

Bo warned him.

"I'm telling you, by herself."

"A girl runs two territories by herself? She don't look like she running the streets dressed for Miami. The chick got on stilettos, her nails and feet are perfectly manicured. You mean to tell me y'all Jersey niggas allowing a bitch to run y'all streets?"

"She has front people and enforcers. It's not like she moves by herself. She pushes mad weight, has the best prices. She makes sure everybody eats. They love us, man!"

"Who is us?" Kay asked.

"The team. We move as a team. We made up a boss that we answer to, they don't know who's in charge, and it's been working for us."

"Who is us?" This time it was Trae wanting to know who this *us* was.

"Me and her."

"You and her? Who's her father?"

"Her father? I don't know. She said she left home when she was almost seventeen. She said her pops is a bad dude who accused her of stealing from him, and he put a hit out on her because she knows too much. She said she stayed in fear of her life for almost three years."

"Did she steal from him?" I asked.

"No. I don't know for real. Y'all know bitches tell us only what they want to. She said she didn't, but I don't know. She n-n-never talks about him." Kevin was sweating and stuttering.

"How did you meet her?" Trae asked.

"I was doing a little something something in Trenton. I had got with this OG, Tracey

Syphax. He introduced us. I sold to her a few times. Then a few months later, she offered to sell to me, and we been getting money ever since."

"You didn't think anything was—hold up, hold up. I gotta take this call. Get him out of here," Kay said.

I think it was the call that he was waiting for. Bo rushed Kev up the stairs, and Kay put the call on speaker. We all gathered around the table. This shit gave me a rush. It had to be the Don.

Tasha

I was getting this Lolita chick to let her guard down just a little when Kevin came racing into the living room and went outside, damn near knocking the door off its hinges. Lolita and I jumped up at the same time and went after him.

"Let me talk to my sister. Take Carlos back into the house. I'll be there in a few," Kevin said as soon as he stepped on the porch. He was pacing back and forth, his shaky hand fumbling to light a blunt.

Lolita glared at him as Carlos tried to squirm down. She turned her now icy gaze on me but was speaking to him. "You sure you don't need me?"

"Nah. This is a family matter. Get your shit together, though. We're about to be out of here." She turned and went back into the house.

"What's going on, Kevin? What did you do?"

"What did *I* do? Them motherfuckers just put a gun to my head!"

"For what? What did you do?"

"They said I'm trying to set them up."

"Set them up? Set them up how?"

"You don't have to yell. According to *your* husband, me bringing Lolita here was a setup."

"Boy, you are not making any sense to me. What does that mean?"

"The fuck if I know. Ask *them*."

"Come on, baby, we're ready. Nice meeting you, Tasha."

Like what you've read?

GO NOW TO WCLARKPUBLISHING.COM

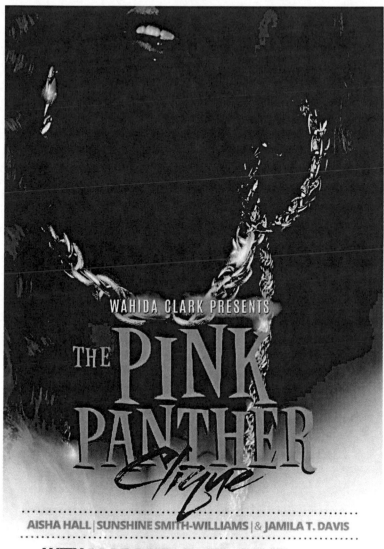

WAHIDA CLARK PRESENTS

The Pink Panther Clique:
Sneak Peek

By

Aisha Hall, Sunshine Smith-Williams,

Jamila T. Davis with Wahida Clark

Wahida Clark Presents Publishing
60 Evergreen Place
Suite 904A
East Orange, New Jersey 07018
1(866)-910-6920
www.wclarkpublishing.com

Library of Congress Cataloging-In-Publication Data:

Aisha Hall, Sunshine Smith-Williams, Jamila T. Davis

Pink Panther Clique Preview

ISBN 13-digit 978-1936649556 (paperback)
ISBN 13-digit 978-1936649730 (ebook)
ISBN 13-digit: 978-1936649709 (Hardback)
LCCN: 2017904236

1. New York, NY - 2. Money Laundering 3. Hip Hop- 4. African American-Fiction- 5. Music Industry- 6. Federal Prisoners-

Cover design and layout by Nuance Art, LLC
Book design by NuanceArt@aCreativeNuance.com
Edited by Linda Wilson
Proofreader Alanna Boutin
Printed in USA

Prologue

She swallowed a basketball. Her big, pregnant belly protruded, giving off that impression.

"There's no way she should *still* be pregnant. She looks like she's about to drop that load any day now," Sun-Solé, a short, voluptuous, caramel-toned woman with long, straight hair said.

"Shhh. Girl, they're going to hear us. Just keep mopping," Eshe warned. She was a tall, chinky-eyed, brown-skinned girl with a strong New York swagger.

"I can't believe y'all got me down here," Milla said. She was a bright-eyed, almond-toned diva who, even in prison, kept her clothes crisp and her makeup on fleek.

The three women watched from a distance as the pregnant girl wobbled to her seat in the visiting room. They pretended to be cleaning, but they were there for a completely different reason. Sun-Solé was the main one who insisted they volunteer as prison orderlies today, because she could smell drama in the air.

"I'm telling y'all," Sun-Solé said, "I heard Prego on the phone. Baby daddy is coming today. Shit's gonna hit the fan, word to mutha."

Milla rolled her eyes at Sun-Solé. She found it funny to see her prison sister with a mop in her hand because, on the contrary, Sun-Solé was a grown-ass princess. Milla knew how her girl truly lived. Maids and assistants did everything at her home, and she never lifted a finger. Sun-Solé's domestic act had Milla chuckling to herself. Those who only knew her in prison would assume Sun-Solé was a regular Suzy Homemaker who took every cleaning job the prison offered. Anything to get her off the cell block and onto Gossip Street. Sun-Solé cleaned every place from the warden's office to the guards' locker room. Then she'd report all that was going on in the prison to Eshe and Milla. She even knew what was happening in the men's facility. But that was an entirely different story.

Sun-Solé, Eshe, and Milla's eyes were like three sharp surveillance cameras, recording every moment, each of them looking on for various reasons. Sun-Solé was the entertainer. She thought everything was a movie, but instead of it being on the big-screen, she watched things play out in real time. Life was one big reality show to her. She took in the whole scene of Prego with her baby daddy and got high from the action of it all.

Milla watched because she wanted to write about every single injustice that was done to each woman in the prison system. She wanted to tear it down, brick by brick, one story at a time, and end mass incarceration once and for all. She hated the American so-called criminal justice system with a passion because it destroyed families. Specifically, women.

Eshe was extremely unconventional. The female corporate thug, a walking almanac who could probably tell you what the weather was like on any given day in the sixth century. The pragmatic one of the group, Eshe moved when driven by logic only and tried to intervene in situations where she could be of help by adding her opinion. Sometimes, it worked; other times, she had to get a bit ratchet and remind chicks where she was from. Eshe got along with everyone, for the most part, but would buck on the guards at any moment.

All of the ladies were from New York, and they moved with a different swag. They observed Prego on the DL, to see how she would get out of the situation. Prego was just a nickname for the pregnant girl whom they'd been observing. Prego's boyfriend stared her down with a confused look.

"This doesn't feel right. You denied my visits all this time. This shouldn't be the first time I'm seeing you. You won't call me. I'm starting to lose my mind. And look at you; you're as big as a house. This doesn't add up. How can you possibly still be pregnant?"

"You don't understand."

"You've been locked up for ten months and two weeks. You found out you were pregnant before you got here. What the hell is going on? I mean, you need to see a specialist—something! You're going to explode. This shit ain't normal," Prego's boyfriend said.

"There's something I need to tell you." Prego did not look at her man. She stared at the floor as if looking for a quick escape. But there was no escaping reality. At least, not for the ladies in Danbury Federal Prison.

"Well, what is it, baby? It's bad enough you're in here

carrying my first child. Is there some type of medical condition I need to know about?" he asked, raising his hands and shaking his head. His perplexed expression caused all three spies to immediately label him as stupid. It didn't matter that he was an attorney. He was a plain ol' dumb ass.

"Visitation is over!" the officer yelled out. "Emergency lockdown. I repeat, visitation is over."

"Awww, shit," one of the spies whispered. "Damn. It's about to go down. Lieutenant Longwood is walking toward them. Look, girl!" Sun-Solé was so excited to see what was about to unfold. Milla was ready to go, and F.she was in protection mode.

Lieutenant Longwood stepped in front of Prego and her man. "Do you all not hear well? Visitation is over."

"As far as I know, according to policy, visits trump all other prison matters. I'm an attorney. I'm seeing my pregnant fiancée for the first time in months. Can you just give us a minute?" Prego still looked at the floor.

"I don't care what *you* do, but her . . . *She* is going back to her unit, now!" Then he did the unthinkable: he grabbed Prego by her arm and lifted her from her seat. Then he whispered something in her ear. A tear fell from her eye.

"Hey, don't put your hands on her like that. Man, are you crazy?" Prego's baby daddy said. Lieutenant Longwood released her arm and folded his own arms across his chest.

"You got *one* minute!"

"Baby, does this man do this often? I am going to file a complaint," he said in a low tone.

69

"Don't bother. I'm stuck here. They do what they want."

"Time's up!" Longwood stated.

"Can I at least give her a kiss? Damn!"

"Hell, no!" he said. "As a matter of fact, Inmate Gaines, don't you have something to tell this clown?"

"Clown? Man, what the fuck is your issue?"

"Not now, Longwood. I'll tell him next time," Prego said.

"Next time? There won't be a next time. You need to let him know, or I will. Today is my last day here, so it needs to be done." She nodded and another tear fell from her eye.

"Okay, I'm gonna just come out and say it."

"Say what?" Baby Daddy asked.

"I'm with Lieutenant Longwood. This is his baby, not yours." Milla, Eshe, and Sun-Solé's mouths dropped open.

"This shit ain't right!" Eshe whispered.

"Well, what the hell are we supposed to do?" Milla added.

"Nothing. What can we do?" Sun-Solé said. By this time, none of them were even pretending to clean. They were just watching. The visiting room was damn near empty, so there was nobody else around to see what was going down.

It was only for a second that they'd looked at each other to speak, but a second was all it took for chaos to break out. By the time they looked back at the love triangle, Baby Daddy was swinging at Lieutenant Longwood. He snuffed the homie.

Crack!

Longwood's jaw fractured. At least that's what it sounded like. Longwood removed his flashlight and caught Baby

Daddy in the head. He fell backward. An alarm sounded, and correction officers were every-damn-where. They were pulling Longwood off of Baby Daddy, and another group had pushed the spies to the corner.

Then suddenly there was a piercing cry. "My stomach!" Prego called out. "Oh God! I think my water broke!" The fight was broken up, and medical workers were paged. Milla, Eshe, and Sun-Solé broke through the human barricade of guards who were guarding them in the corner and ran to Prego.

"It's going to be all right," Eshe said, sitting Prego onto the floor.

"No, it's not," she whispered. "This baby ain't neither one of theirs!"

"What! Who's the father?" Eshe asked.

More guards arrived in the visiting room, and they ordered the three spies to get up against the wall so they could be cuffed and taken back to their unit. Sun-Solé was ear hustling. Her hearing was on high alert like a bunny's ears. But nobody heard anything because there was too much noise and chaos. There was blood everywhere from both Lieutenant Longwood and Baby Daddy. Eshe turned around one last time to look at Prego, and she quickly mouthed one name to her. A name they all knew.

Nahhhhh. It can't be! The scandal was deeper than anyone could have ever imagined, and shit was about to hit the fan!

* * * *

Chapter 1

Milla

♫ *You the only one I love (uh-huh)/The only man I know that I can trust (yup)/And if I ever should need you, I know you'll come (yeah) ready to kill with a smoking gun (with a smoking gun).* ♫

I sang passionately to Jadakiss's song "Smoking Gun." The words made me think about love and how it used to feel. But at this very moment, the most important thing on my mind was money. I put L. Boogie, Jill Scott, and Adele on rotation to keep me in my zone. Until my office phone rang and interrupted me. After five rings, I picked up. My boss's extension showed on the display in big, black digital numbers.

"Yes, Mr. Darding," I answered.

"Ms. Davison, I need to see you in my office . . . pronto!"

"Sure thing." I hung up and sat there awhile. Although he was my boss, I wasn't the type of employee who asked how high when a higher-up told me to jump. After I was good and ready, I turned my music off and got into professional mode. Professional mode was something that came natural to me, but so did my street persona.

By the way, my name is Jamila Davison, but I go by the name of Milla. I work for Standard American Bank, also known as SAB, one of the largest banks in the country. Currently, I'm a loan agent, and I've got the best track record in our district. I close millions of dollars' worth of loans every single month, and my numbers are steadily increasing. In other words, I'm a beast when it comes to finance. But once I left the office and got into the comfort of my whip, I opened my ashtray, lit up some bud, and blasted Jadakiss. I knew how to turn it on and off. It was a survival mechanism that I'd learned over the years while growing up in Queens. I am who I am, a true black woman who loves her culture. I could pick up a mic and spit a verse with the dudes I grew up with, or I could pick up a mic and sell our bank's latest loan products to a crowd of investors. Because I was equipped with a skill set that allowed me to indulge in the best of both worlds, I was a true chameleon. I grew up not missing a beat in the streets, but also staying on top of my schooling. I was sure my persona would take me far, and I would soon find out just how far once I walked into Mr. Darding's office.

"Ms. Davison. How are you?" he said upon me entering.

"I'm fine. How about you, sir?" I replied, shaking his hand.

"Good, good. Have a seat." I sat my well-rounded booty in the comfort of the black leather chair in front of his desk. He adjusted his seat so he could keep an eye on my legs. And like a salivating dog, he licked his lips as I crossed one leg over the other. *Men. So damn predictable.* It took everything in me to not burst out laughing. Darding was about fifty-five years old, partially bald, with an oversized gut. I didn't give a damn how much money he had; I would never bounce up and down on his lap. Never. Ugh! But still, I smiled, anxious to know what he wanted from me.

"Is everything all right? I see that you wanted me to come here right away. I can't say I'm not nervous. Being called into the principal's office is not always a good thing." He laughed.

"Milla. May I call you Milla?"

"Sure. I prefer it actually. We're all family here at SAB." I threw on the charm, but I wished he would get to the damn point.

"Well, you're here because today is a very special day for you. There's something we noticed about you."

I cleared my throat. "Like what?"

"Most of the clients whom you've been giving loans to are rappers and other famous African Americans. Also, you've been bringing in other individuals who are . . . ummm, let's just say, not the *typical* clients we see come into our bank. Or any bank for that matter." He chuckled at his own joke. I did not. Then I started to think about this impromptu meeting . . . *Awww, shit. If he's going to fire me, he needs to just get to it and stop horsing around. I put a lot of blood, sweat, and tears into this bank. Hell, I brought in new business however I could. So if they're trying to get rid of me, I got a few choice words for his ass!*

So here is the raw truth about how I played the banking game: I just happened to see an opportunity with these celebrities and wanted to help them while helping myself. I had to pull teeth sometimes to get them approved for loans. I even had to tell little white lies sometimes because a lot of them didn't have tax returns or had cash businesses. But what I did was still good. Helping guys with new record deals get their first Bentley, Maybach, Rolls-Royce, or Lamborghini. Taking dope boys from the projects to gated communities. So what, I made up pay stubs. They paid their bills, and that was all that mattered. I was making the bank lots of money because all my people paid their loans back. They better had, or else they would have to deal with me personally. I figured I would sell myself before he gave me the bad news. You know, try to save face.

"I just spoke with Jadakiss. He's a famous rapper right here in New York, and he was approved for a $2 million mortgage not too long ago. I got him to put a million down, so he's well invested. I can tell you, I know him personally, and he will not only pay, but pay early. And Zab Judah, five-time champion boxer, he just paid off a $3.5 million loan that I worked very hard to get for him. I know my methods were a little nontraditional, but my goal is to make this bank #1 in the world. The world, sir. No other bank could do it, but I got it done. If there is something wrong with the—" He interrupted me.

"No, there is nothing wrong. Actually, we think what you're doing is great. You're bringing in some unusual characters, yes, and it's making the bank a lot of money. There is some good news that recently came down the pipeline." He leaned in closer from his side of the desk. "We want to promote you. We want you to bring more of your, uh, your people into our establishment. It's a win-win situation for all of us." He got up and closed his office door, then sat back down and talked in a hushed tone.

"I know a lot of these rapper characters don't have good credit, Milla. We also noticed you seem to know a lot of . . ."—now he went into an all-out whisper—"drug dealers and street guys. But they still have plenty of money, and we can still sell houses to these people. We just need you and your wit to help continue to bridge that gap. We'll give you whatever you need. There is just one condition."

"Okay . . . and what's that?" His breath stank of the rotten bullshit that was about to fly out of his mouth any second. *Here it comes.*

"Well, all of these types of loans need to start with 14 percent interest."

"Fourteen percent?" I repeated, shocked. I looked at him as if he'd passed me the whip and asked me to beat his slaves for him. He'd lost his mind. My stare lingered. *He can't be serious. That amount is outrageous!* I was about to get up and walk out, but I pondered his offer briefly. Yeah, he thought he was getting over by exploiting my people, giving them high interest loans that any knowledgeable person would never pay. However, I saw an opportunity to help a lot of people, and my brain had already started churning out a plan to get around that interest rate crap. I could work my magic once I got an opportunity to get creative. And it sounded like he was giving me that power.

"What exactly would the position be?"

"Special accounts manager."

"And the meaning of *special*?" I asked, raising a freshly waxed eyebrow.

"Well, we'll leave that to you. We can get creative. But, of course, we want the bank to be known for bridging the gap and giving minorities opportunities that no other bank has done. And the best part of it is: we'll give you your own team with underwriting power to approve loans up to $5 million! We've got about $500 million to lend. Who knows, you can be the Oprah Winfrey savior for your people. Think about what you can do. Not just for yourself, but for your community." Never in America does a bank suddenly tell a black person they have access to so much money, to give to more black folks. *Something is off with this. This is corporate America, and we aren't welcome here.*

"Of course, I'll accept. I love it! Thank you so much for the opportunity, Mr. Darding." We shook on it. My name was already ringing bells. I surely didn't want to sound off any alarms. If I felt that he was up to something crazy, I would back out. But I'd wait until that happened, if ever.

I exited the bank, jumped in my Benz, and celebrated with a fat-ass blunt. Yeah, Milla Winfrey had a crazy ring to it! But I also found out that if something sounded too good to be true . . . it usually was!

Like what you've read?

GO NOW TO WCLARKPUBLISHING.COM

WAHIDA CLARK PRESENTS

Pretty Boy Hustlerz

Sneak Peek

By

Victor L. Martian

Pretty Boy Hustlerz

Wahida Clark Presents Publishing
60 Evergreen Place
Suite 904A
East Orange, New Jersey 07018
1(866)-910-6920
www.wclarkpublishing.com

Library of Congress Cataloging-In-Publication Data:

Victor L. Martin

Pretty Boy Hustlerz

ISBN 13-digit 978-1944992767 (paperback)
ISBN 13-digit 978-1944992835 (ebook)
ISBN 13-digit: 978-1944992798 (Hardback)
LCCN: 2017904236

1. North Carolina- 3. Drug Trafficking- 4. African American-Fiction- 5. Urban Fiction- 6. State Prisons- 7. Pretty boy

Cover design and layout by Nuance Art, LLC
Book design by NuanceArt@aCreativeNuance.com
Edited by Linda Wilson

Printed in USA

Chapter One

Selma, North Carolina

June 11th, Tuesday
Present Time

"I can't keep living like this, Lorenzo!" Shayla Graham shouted with tears filling her eyes. She wiped them and stared at her boyfriend from across the bedroom.

"Do you know what I got in the mail today? More bills! Overdue bills that you promised to help me with. Every month you have a new excuse with your half of the bills. The rent is behind. My car is about to be repossessed. And nearly every damn night I have to feed our son some needles!"

"You act like I don't have no bills of my own!" Lorenzo fired back.

"What bills! How the hell you gonna convince me that you need some chrome rims on your cars?" She yelled. "We're about to be homeless! And all you do is front like shit is sweet when you know our shit is fucked up. You can't be like, Travis and rip and run the streets and blow money. What you need to do is maintain your home like a real man is supposed to!"

"Ain't trying to be like Travis!" Lorenzo shoved his arm

81

through the ironed sleeves of his uniform.

"I can't tell!" Shayla glared at Lorenzo. "Ever since you got that job at the prison you've been trying to do what Travis do. FYI Travis doesn't have the responsibilities that you have. You have a son Lorenzo. We're about to lose everything baby. If I have to move back to Smithfield with my mom, where will you go? What? Back up to Michigan with your family."

"I'm doing the best I can, Shayla! I can't give you what I don't have."

"Something has to change. And it has to be now. Every damn day I'm having to beg for overtime at Walmart and nine times out of ten I never get it. I can't keep giving you gas money when my own damn tank stays on empty."

"It's not like I'm not trying, Shayla." He turned to face her. "I hate being broke all the time and living from check to check."

Shayla flopped down on the foot of the bed with her chin down. "This is driving me crazy! Why is this happening to me? It's the same problems every month," she murmured. "If I lose this home, I don't know what will become of us, Lorenzo."

"Shayla," Lorenzo called out.

"What?" She looked up.

"Baby, I know times are hard. But you have to believe in me. Have some faith in me."

"Believing in you and having faith in you isn't going to keep a roof over our heads. I swear I'm trying to stick this one out with you." Shayla softened her tone.

"Times get hard and you wanna break up!"

"I didn't say that," she replied.

"So, what was that shit about you not knowing what will become of us!"

Her eyes began to pool with fresh tears. She crossed her arms and looked down at the floor, slightly rocking back and forth. *Maybe I would be better off by myself. Just my son and I. But God, I love Lorenzo*, she thought with a hurting heart.

"Talk to me, Shayla. Where all this breaking up bullshit coming from? Over some fucking bills?"

"It's not just some fucking bills!" she snapped. "It's us, Lorenzo! Our life. Our present and our future. But you know what?" she shot to her feet and glared at him. "I'm willing to do whatever to keep this place our home! If I have to—" she paused to wipe her tears. "I'll go to Wilson and work out—"

"No the fuck you ain't!" Lorenzo butted in. "That bullshit ain't even up for discussing! You can dead that idea and I mean it, Shayla!"

"But."

"No! I meant what I said, Shayla. I'll figure something out, okay."

Shayla bit her tongue on the job opportunity in Wilson. Beefing with Lorenzo wasn't helping her issue. She no longer cared what he wanted to discuss or not. Shayla had a fix to ease the issue of her bills, and at this point, she felt cornered into doing it behind Lorenzo's back.

***

Lorenzo Watson arrived at Maury Correctional Institution with his troubles still pressing. The only good thing so far was being posted in the control booth from 6 p. m. to 10 p. m. Since lockdown was called at 11:00 p. m., it would only be one hour of dealing with the worrisome ass inmates. From his seat in the booth he could see all three blocks, A, B, and C. Each block held forty-eight grown men, but in Watson's view, it was nothing but a fucking day care center. For the next twelve hours, his goal was to sit on his ass and do next to nothing. He never gave the inmates a hard time and he was known to turn a blind eye on a number of wrong doings. As long as they weren't trying to kill each other or escape, Watson stayed in his lane. All he wanted was his two checks a month and that was it. Around 9:00 p. m., operations made the announcement to lockdown for count. As always it was ignored by 90% of the inmates. They wouldn't move from the card table or TV's until an officer came inside the block. Watson could've been an ass by turning the TV's off but that wasn't his temper. The three floor officers and the sergeant started with C block to lockdown. For the next few minutes, Watson had to respond to his radio and pop the cells open for each inmate to lockdown. The task was the norm to Watson, dull and boring to be honest. When all of the dorms were cleared he scanned the control board to make sure all of the cell doors were secured.

"All cell doors are secured for A, B, and C dorms," Watson said over the radio.

"Ten-four," Sergeant Karen Parker replied.

Watson reached for his soda when the phone rung inside the booth. "North side control," he answered.

"What's up, Watson? You in the booth again tonight?" Officer Lisa Hart asked.

"Yeah and I hope to stay up here. What's up with you down there?"

"Just wrote up one of these nasty ass clowns down here jacking off on me in the shower! Wrote his natural black ass right on up! I hate that nasty shit!"

Watson laughed, "Who was it?"

"Um…Charles Pender in F-block. Seriously, not that I would fuck an inmate but damn, what happened to all these men with the solid talk game? First moment these fools see a woman in the booth they fly up to the shower and leave the curtain wide the fuck open. I see enough dick at home. Shit burns me the fuck up!" Hart griped.

"What time you gonna take your break?" Watson asked after Hart finished venting.

"Uh… around midnight. Why? What's up?"

"Just asking. Oh, where Dixon at?"

"Mr. Travis Dixon is in F-block locking the kids down which is taking forever because he's too laid back."

"Tell 'im to come holler at me after count."

"Boy, please. Y'all two are like brothers. You already know his ass will be down there to see you. But I'll relay the message anyway."

"Okay, thanks."

"Oh, and guess who got walked out yesterday on the other

85

shift?"

"Who?"

"Williamson up on green unit."

"Word! Talking 'bout the white girl with black hair?"

"Yep. Her dumpy ass got caught in the storage room with the canteen man."

"Damn! How she get caught up?"

"From the inmate running his fucking mouth! He told one too many of his homeboys and one of 'em dropped a letter on his ass. She also was dumb enough to send dude some nude pics to his cell phone that was found in his cell. I tell ya, a man in prison will fuck any woman breathing. Now I know I can stand to lose a few pounds myself…but ole girl was obese!" Officer Hart rambled.

"Will she be charged?"

"I doubt it but her fat ass is out of a job that's for damn sure. I guess she couldn't handle all the attention she got in here and fell for the first line of game thrown in her direction. I ain't listening to none of the bullshit these fools in here trying to spit. Fuck that. Motherfuckers can't pay my rent or car note, ain't talking 'bout shit, and that's just keeping it real!"

"True." Watson nodded.

"Well lemme get my ass off this phone so I can call my girl over on red unit."

It's because we got an empty refrigerator. Watson thought. "Thanks, Hart and I mean that."

Watson ended the call with Hart aka Miss Gossip Queen.

She was cool and easy to deal with and had trained Watson when he first started working. She was in her mid-forties, married with two kids and having an affair with Dixon. Plus she favored Oprah Winfrey.

At 9:23 p. m., Watson wrote in the logbook that the count was cleared. The control board lit up as each inmate pressed their call button for their cell door to be popped. It was an easy task, pressing a button beside each blinking red light. It took Watson under two minutes to let everyone out. Watching the monitor he saw the feminine guy in B-block sliding inside another man's cell. Up on the top tier, an inmate was gestured for the shower to be turned on. Watson flipped the switch for all the showers, then leaned back in the chair. Nothing hard at all about his job. Thinking of his troubles he realized he still had a better life than the 144 inmates in the three blocks. Any one of them would trade places to be free without a second thought. Watson had to come up with a plan to earn more money to keep his life together.

His pride took a beating by Shayla's words but all she had spoken was the truth. He had a family to support and was worried if he could man up to it. His first line of thinking centered around pulling overtime. It would force him to deal with that dumb ass, straight-laced sergeant on B-rotation. Slumped in the chair he tried to keep it together when Dixon entered the booth at 9:50 p. m.

Dixon and Watson were indeed the best of friends. Dixon had been a CO at MCI for five years and by all accounts, he loved his job. Both were on their pretty boy swag. At the age

87

of twenty-four, Watson's dark tone and forever fresh haircut placed him in favor of Trey Songz. Travis, two years older, had a much lighter tone from his mixed race genes, set in likeness to Drake. Both stood at six feet even with an average build that suited their frames.

"Damn I'm tired," Dixon flopped down on a gray plastic chair beside Watson. He wore his state-issued Department of Public Safety cap like a fitted over his waves.

"I don't see how 'cause you ain't done shit." Watson joked.

"This unit couldn't run without me and you know it."

"Yeah right."

"You just mad because I get to do my own thang up in here," Dixon grinned.

"Hell, you fucking Hart so that shouldn't be a big ass surprise."

"Whoa bruh," Dixon smiled. "Check it, I don't *fuck* Hart... I only have sex with 'er so get it right. Now with my jump off, I fucks her sweet ass every chance I get and the pussy is hella good. For real, Asian girls do it better."

"That's TMI for me." Watson laughed. "I just hope you don't get caught up in your ways."

"Man, fuck them hoes. Why were you looking all spaced out in line up? Something wrong?"

Watson sighed. If there was anyone he could rap with and keep it 100, it was Dixon. "I might need to put in for some overtime to make ends meet. Bills are piling up on me, bruh."

"Shayla still working?" Dixon wondered. *With her fine*

ass! Dixon secretly lusted.

"Yeah. But her checks ain't what they used to be," Watson complained.

"I'm glad I don't have any kids. Word up, I keep my shit covered all the time. But anyway how much are you behind with your bills?" Dixon asked as he removed his cap.

Watson scratched his chin. "'Round like five thousand."

"Man, working on B-rotation is gonna stress you the fuck out. Sergeant Miles ain't worth shit," Dixon stated.

"Ain't got no other choice, bruh. I got a family to support so all that other shit, I'll just have to deal with it and do me."

Dixon figured Watson's issues were bad since he had lent him a few dollars for lunch last week. "Man, if you do that they might move you to B-rotation since they are already short of staff. *Yeah. Get moved to B-rotation so I can dip over on the low to Shayla. Man, I'd love to see that tight little ass in a thong!*

"It don't matter yo. I got no other choice. I figure I can swing a couple of overtime shifts to get over this ditch 'til I get back on my feet. I'ma talk to Parker on my break and see what's up."

"Don't do it," Dixon shook his head. *Yeah, do it. Shayla don't need your broke ass anyway.*

"What! Are you listening, bruh? Shit is fucking crazy at home and my money is looking funny so–"

"Bruh, you have another choice." *Shit! I might as well help him out.*

"Oh yeah? Where?" Watson looked all around the booth

then threw his arms up in the air.

"Can I trust you?" Dixon lowered his voice with a serious expression.

Watson crossed his arms. "What do you think? And how does that matter about the fact of me needing money?"

"Why do you think I like this job so much?"

Watson shrugged. "Is it these low self-esteem women you be chasing?"

"Fuck no!" Dixon stood. "Bruh, I'ma put you up on game 'cause I fucks with you. No bullshit... I trap this money every day up in this bitch."

Watson frowned. "You ain't on the block no more, bruh, and I'm talking about the streets. In a few eyes... we the fucking police... the man. Listen to what the inmates yell when we make rounds in the blocks. 'Block is hot. Man down.' So how are you trapping?"

Dixon's pride pushed him to prove Watson wrong. Once his pride was mixed with his ego it was a wrap. "How you think guys up in here be failing those drug tests and shit?"

"What does it have to do with me because I really don't care?"

"It can have a lot to do with you if you're tired of being short on money. Listen, I told you I was renting them rims on my Lac right? Well, I paid for them the same day with cash."

Watson shifted in his chair not understanding why Dixon had lied. "Those Rucci rims cost three stacks–"

"And I paid cash." Dixon cut in.

"Okay, you don't have bills like I do so you can–"

"That ain't the point, bruh. When I said I'm trapping, that's what I mean. This job is a gold mine and you don't even see it. When they took tobacco out of prison it was a blessing."

"How?" Watson was curious.

Dixon sat back down. "So I can trust you?"

Watson was hooked on how Dixon made money behind bars. The lure of easing the weight of his money issues was too tempting to let pass. If Dixon could spend $3,000 for a set of rims, then Watson wanted to do the same. "Yeah you can trust me. Now tell me what you got baking."

Like what you've read?
GO NOW TO WCLARKPUBLISHING.COM

WAHIDA CLARK PRESENTS

Black Senate

Sneak Peek

By

Zaid Za'hid

Black Senate

This is a work of fiction. Names, characters, places, and incidents either are the product of the author's imagination or are used fictitiously, and any resemblance to actual persons, living or dead, business establishments, events, or locales are entirely coincidental.

Wahida Clark Presents Publishing
60 Evergreen Place
Suite 904A
East Orange, New Jersey 07018
1(866)-910-6920
www.wclarkpublishing.com

Library of Congress Cataloging-In-Publication Data:

ISBN 13-digit 978-1944992-54-5 (paperback)
ISBN 13-digit 978-1944992569 (ebook)
ISBN 13-digit: 978-1944992552 (Hardback)
LCCN: 2017904233

1. Crime 2. Drug Trafficking- 3. African Americans-Fiction-
4. Urban Fiction- 5. Mafia- 6. Chicago-

Cover design and layout by Nuance Art, LLC
Book design by NuanceArt@aCreativeNuance.com
Edited by Linda Wilson

Printed in USA

94

I
PENITENTIARY CHANCES
CHAPTER ONE

Dressed in all black, Malachi, YaYa, and Jerusalem sat around a chestnut brown table loading and checking their automatic weapons. The crew had graduated from just young hustlers to controlling their own turf. If it came down to it, they killed for their respect with no hesitation. They quickly got a reputation and a name for themselves. Some even called them the BBB—Bad Black Brothas.

Inside the rundown apartment, one of the most notorious projects in Chicago, they passed the blunt around as Tupac's song, "Get Money" played in the background. Jerusalem recited on beat, ". . . today I make a killing . . ." He stopped rapping so they could go over their plan to rob First National Bank.

If they pulled off the heist, they would have enough money to increase their drug supply and expand their organization. This would eliminate some of their competitors. The old heads in the drug game were not showing Jerusalem and his crew any love. They hated to see the young soldiers moving up so rapidly, and they wouldn't let Jerusalem score from them. When they did let Jerusalem score, they almost doubled the prices on the product, making it hard for him to profit. So Jerusalem came up with a plan. With an inside connection, he, along with his crew, planned to hold up one of the largest banks in the city. If he possessed more money, he could bypass the old heads and one day get close enough to kill them all. This was the day they were to put their plan in action.

Jerusalem turned toward Malachi and said, "Remember, your job is to hold off the guard, but without killing him."

Malachi, with dreads that barely sat on his shoulders, responded, "If anyone flinches, I'm shooting. I'm not hesitating to plug their ass."

"Just don't get trigger happy, 'cause I know you have a hair trigger finger. If it's not necessary to commit a murder in this robbery, then don't do it. Our whole mission is to go in, get this money, and come out. We got two minutes to do this from the time we enter the bank," Jerusalem said.

"Where Pinky's yellow ass at?" YaYa asked.

"You know she's always late. That bitch will be late for her own funeral because her stupid ass would be trying to put her own make-up on," Malachi said.

They all laughed but got quiet when they heard the secret knock—two taps and a pause then one tap and a pause and three taps. Malachi jumped up and opened the door. "Bitch, where you been?"

"You think stealing a SUV is easy," Pinky, the streetwise and curvaceous eighteen year old said while rolling her neck with lots of attitude. "Jerusalem told me specifically to get a

96

dark SUV. Motherfucker, I had my girl drive me all over Chimney Hills this morning before I found one." Her role in the heist was only to be the get-a-way driver.

Jerusalem eyed the 5-feet 5-inches tall, big, emerald eyed beauty in the tight fitting jeans she loved to wear to show off her body. Her heart-shaped head was filled with long, dark curly hair drawn up into a ponytail.

"You're looking beautiful, ma," he said. "What you have on is perfect? 'Cause you're supposed to look like an ordinary patron, a beautiful woman behind the wheel. When we enter the car, we don't want you to do no speeding. Drive the speed limit, because we're going to duck down where it looks like you're the only one in the SUV.

"YaYa, your role is to make sure that all the customers and workers in the bank are under control. Whatever you do, don't let a motherfucka get to their cell phone."

"I got you," YaYa responded.

While talking, they loaded their guns, ski masks, and gloves into one duffel bag.

Jerusalem asked Pinky, "You strapped already?"

Her full-sized, pink lips moved as she replied, "Yes, I keep my man with me." She patted her small waistline to indicate the weapon was securely hidden. With the curves she carried, every hustler in the neighborhood attempted to get their hands on Pinky. Men drooled over her every time they saw her thick hips and ass like Serena Williams.

They exited the project doors.

An hour later, after casing the area one last time, Pinky

pulled the SUV in front of the bank. Jerusalem looked around the area. "Go," he said.

Malachi, pulling the black Spider-Man mask over his head, was the first to exit the SUV. He held the AK-47 assault rifle out as he entered the bank doors. YaYa followed suit, holding a .357 Smith and Wesson with extra bullets around his waist. When he walked, his shirt swayed, revealing the weapon. Jerusalem patted his pocket, confirming he had four extra clips in each one. He tightened his Spider-Man mask down under his chin and extended his .45 automatic weapon as he entered the bank last.

"Everybody get the fuck down!" Malachi yelled. "Don't nobody fucking move!"

It looked as if the security guard was contemplating a move. Malachi immediately put the gun to the white security guard's head and said, "Motherfucka, don't even flinch. If you do, I won't hesitate to put a bullet in your fuckin' head."

YaYa yelled out, "Down on the floor, now! Keep your hands visible where I can see them." He waved the gun near the customers to show he meant business. Some of the customers wailed, but they all obeyed.

Jerusalem jumped over the bank counter with the duffle bag. "You three, on the floor. Now!"

The three women crowded together and whimpered. One sounded like she was hyperventilating as they bent down and got on the floor. Jerusalem ignored them and pointed the gun at the bank manager. "You too."

Only one cashier remained standing, and she was the one

Jerusalem knew.

"A minute and forty-five seconds!" YaYa yelled near the frightened customers.

Jerusalem turned his attention to the cashier and pointed the gun to the side of her head and said, "Bitch, you know what to do. Take me to the money."

Instead of Jerusalem taking her to the cashiers' drawers, he led her to an open safe that held over 200 thousand crisp hundreds and twenties. "This is what I'm talking about," he said as he held one gun on the cashier and used the other hand to load the money.

YaYa shouted, "Sixty seconds!"

Jerusalem forced the cashier to the floor and stuffed as much money as he could into the bag.

"Forty-five seconds!" YaYa yelled, looking at his watch.

Jerusalem pointed the gun at the cashiers and the bank manager. "Get up." He directed them to walk around the counter. "Down. Now!" He demanded them to lie on the floor with the rest of the bank patrons.

Malachi walked the unarmed guard to the same location. "On the floor, motherfucka!"

"Fifteen seconds!" YaYa said.

Jerusalem passed the duffle bag to YaYa, who rushed out of the bank first and hopped into the SUV. He was unaware of the off duty undercover officer who happened to be in the area. The officer was entering the restaurant next door but stopped when he saw YaYa exit the bank.

Malachi exited next and climbed in the back of the SUV.

They both kneeled down in the backseat.

Jerusalem, with his eyes still on the people on the floor, held his weapon in their direction, while backing up toward the door.

Pinky kept the SUV running, and was first to notice the plain-clothes officer. When he reached for his gun, she saw the sunlight reflect off the metal badge on his belt. "There go a motherfuckin' cop!" she yelled.

As Jerusalem backed up out the bank, the cop yelled, "Freeze, motherfucka, and slowly put down your weapon!"

Jerusalem turned and faced the cop with his weapon drawn. "No, you drop your weapon."

"Drop your fuckin' weapon now!" the cop demanded.

"No, you drop your weapon!" Jerusalem replied calmly.

Pinky roared the engine to signal to Jerusalem that it was time to move out. Both the officer and Jerusalem turned their head toward the SUV. Malachi was in the backseat with the AK47 pointed at the off duty cop. Jerusalem eyed Pinky. Pinky looked at Jerusalem.

"Go!" Jerusalem said.

Pinky hesitated as sirens wailed in the distance. Water filled Pinky's eyes. She didn't want to leave him, but Jerusalem yelled out, "Bitch, did you hear what I said? Go!"

Thinking Malachi was ready to fire at any second, YaYa pulled down Malachi's arm and said, "We got the money. No need for that. Jerusalem can take care of himself."

Malachi bit down on his bottom lip and reasoned with himself as YaYa told Pinky, "Drive, baby girl!"

Pinky smashed on the gas, dodging the bullets the officer fired toward the SUV. She sped off into oncoming traffic.

Jerusalem, using himself as a sacrifice to save his crew, set off running. A foot chase got underway. He dodged in and out between cars and turned a corner, hoping it would lead to an escape route to freedom. Two police cars sped out of nowhere and blocked his way. He turned and the plain-clothes officer was still coming fast behind him. He slipped in a shop and ran through the store knocking down items. Customers in the store screamed as he ran toward the back of the store looking for an exit door.

Pushing the door open, he ran down the alley away from the main street, while taking off his mask with one hand. He jumped over the wall as his heart beat out of control. Jerusalem hoped he'd lost the cops pursuing him. The moment he looked up, a group of officers were pointing their guns directly at him. He bent down and placed his weapon on the ground just in case a trigger happy cop was in their midst. Defeated, he lifted both hands in the air as the officers ordered him to the ground.

One of the officers rushed over to him and yelled, "Put your hands behind your back! You're under arrest!"

Tired and exhausted, Jerusalem did as ordered. The officer said, "You have the right to remain silent," as he picked Jerusalem up from the ground.

Jerusalem held his head back and closed his eyes as the officer continued to read him the Miranda rights.

The sound of the lock clicking brought Jerusalem back

into present day—eight years after the bank heist.

Being in solitary confinement was a mental battle that Jerusalem Williams was determined to win. Dressed in just his boxers, he lay on the hard concrete floor of the jail cell with his hands locked behind his head staring up at the ceiling.

Like what you've read?

GO NOW TO WCLARKPUBLISHING.COM

WAHIDA CLARK PRESENTS

SINCERELY, THE BOSS!

Sneak Peek

A Novel By
Wahida Clark & Amy Morford

Wahida Clark Presents Publishing, LLC
60 Evergreen Place
Suite 904
East Orange, New Jersey 07018
1 (866)-910-6920
www.wclarkpublishing.com

ISBN 13-digit 978-1-944992-20-0
ISBN 10-digit 9781944992200
eBook ISBN 978-1-936649-11-2
Audio ISBN: 978-1-936649-08-02

Library of Congress Catalog Number
1.   Urban, 2. Romance 3. Suspense 4. Mafia 5. Italian 6. New York City 7. Crime
Cover design and layout by Nuance Art, LLC
Book interior design by www.aCreativeNuance.com
Contributing Editors: Linda Wilson and R. Hamilton

Printed in United States

Prologue

*M*argo's phone rang, and she shrugged at Carol, as if to apologize for cutting her off. Secretly grateful to have an excuse this time, she saw it was Abby again and wondered if this was an apology.

"Hello, sweetie," she started but Abigail cut her off.

"Did you tell Dad that I wasn't in school?"

Margo could tell she was fuming. It seemed to be her daughter's normal state of emotion where Margo was concerned.

"I did," Margo confirmed. Abigail had been skipping school, and now she would blame her mother for whatever punishment David might dole out.

"I'm sorry, but I was worried about you." She had a million questions for Abby, none of which were going to get answered.

"I hate you!" Abigail screamed into the phone. "I hate you, and I wish you had just stayed in prison."

The line went dead. Margo let out a defeated sigh. She put the phone back in her bag and shrugged her shoulders at Carol.

"Kids!" she muttered to herself.

* * * *

Chapter 1

The alarm clock blared and Margo groaned as she felt for the off button. She glared at the time, a whole four hours of sleep and it was time to start all over again. After a year of working three jobs, sleep was what she longed for. The dreams, however, were a different story. She rolled out of bed, and her feet hit the floor. There was no point in letting herself wallow in her current situation. She might not be an optimist, but if the last seven years had taught her anything, it was that she was as tough as nails.

Margo wrapped the towel around herself after getting out of the shower. Damn, if there was one thing she missed about her house it was taking a long, hot bath in her whirlpool tub after a long day at the office. Living at the motel sucked, even though she didn't spend a lot of time here. The plumbing was old, and showers were either scalding hot or ice cold. This morning, she had chosen frigid over third-degree burns and she was covered in goose bumps. She scowled at her reflection. The worry lines had become permanent recently. She checked her face for any other disconcerting developments. At forty-three, Margo knew that she still turned heads, tall and curvy, with long, auburn hair, and intense, green eyes that were still a distraction for men.

She rolled her eyes; she was a distraction for all the *wrong* kind of men. How long had it been now? No, she didn't have time for fantasy. Reality occupied all of her time, and there was little chance that Prince Charming was going to walk into the diner this morning and, between coffee and the check, offer to whisk her away.

Margo checked her uniform and her backpack before heading out. She would return sometime around midnight, almost comatose, and she would barely get undressed before falling quickly to sleep again. At first when she started this routine, she had told herself that working long hours would help her stay sane. Lately, she wasn't so sure.

She didn't have time to second-guess herself, and that was a blessing. It was three hours into the breakfast shift and the diner was slammed. Margo had waited tables on and off when she was a teenager, but had gone to college so these kinds of menial jobs would be forever in the past. If she could give her own children one piece of advice now, it would be to never say never.

Margo knew it was after nine, but not before ten, because she saw Sal walk in. He strode through the diner like he owned the place, and for all Margo knew, he might have. His dark hair was slicked back neatly; the touches of gray made him look even more distinguished. His suit was impeccable as always. He was the only man that she'd seen in the year she worked here who wore cuff links. She had realized shortly after meeting him though that it wouldn't have mattered what he wore; he exuded a quiet power, and he knew it. The other customers were quiet when he passed by, and he took his usual seat. He always sat in her section.

Her cheeks flushed this morning when she picked up the coffeepot and headed in his direction. She blamed it on the fact that he flirted with her; sometimes she blamed it on the fact that she couldn't remember the last time she had sex, but Sal's attention lately had made her long for a little romance.

"Good morning, Sunshine. How's my favorite customer today?"

She smiled when she saw him. She couldn't help it; he was contagious and had that kind of effect on her with that twinkle of mischief in his eyes.

"Wonderful, Cookie, and how's my favorite waitress faring today?"

His voice was gruff, and if Margo was honest, she imagined him calling her "Cookie" during some intimate moments.

"Great, you want the usual?"

He gave her those smoldering eyes and the look that kept her simmering lately. "If I can't get anything else . . ."

Their banter went back to the day they met, but the flirtation had become more heated lately, and Margo went in the back and eyed him from the kitchen. She had heard the stories; according to Vinnie, the line cook with a lazy eye, Sal was powerful businessman with ties to the Mafia. From her past dealings with the criminal element, she believed it. He was definitely a man who knew how to get what he wanted.

When she returned with Sal's usual, a glass of orange juice, two eggs over easy, and a slice of dry wheat toast, he stopped her. "Hey, Cookie, you're a smart girl, let me ask you something."

"Sure, Sal, anything." It was a lie; Margo was very good at dodging answers.

"What are you doing working here?" He looked around to indicate that the diner might not be a career choice for someone with ambition and half a brain.

Margo shrugged. "I needed a job. Help wanted sign in the window, five-question interview, I fit in the uniform, and voilà. Hired on the spot. Do you need more coffee?"

She was quick to change the subject. No matter how attractive Sal might be and how much they flirted, there were certain subjects that were off-limits.

Her section filled up again quickly, and Margo must have been in the kitchen when Sal left. When she went back to his table and found it empty, she couldn't help but feel slightly disappointed. Sometimes conversation with Sal was just about the only thing that made her smile all day. Under his coffee cup, he had left his usual ten-dollar tip and she folded the money and slid it into her pocket.

At noon, it was time to change and get to her second job. Thankfully, the Laundromat didn't require that she wear a uniform as ridiculous as the getup she wore at the diner. It was far too low-cut and showed way too much leg. Margo had complained to Vinnie.

"I'm not making enough money here to flash cleavage."

"Hey, think about how much less you'd make if you didn't." He had winked at her with his good eye, and she knew that the case was closed.

Jeans and a tee shirt were all she needed for her second job and the peace and quiet there gave her time to work on her third job.

Margo walked the ten blocks from the diner to the Laundromat. This was her only real free time of the day, and she would stop, grab a quick bite from the deli and one more cup of coffee. She had to remind herself to eat lately; she had lost enough weight over the last few years, and there was no point in getting sick. The cell phone in her backpack rang as she was chewing. Margo swallowed quickly. She didn't get many calls.

"Hello?" she answered, clearing her throat. "Hello?" she repeated.

"Hey, Mom." It was Abigail, her daughter who should be in school right now. Margo immediately wondered why she was calling her, what was wrong.

"Honey, are you okay? Are you at school?" Her sweet little girl had grown up way too fast and Margo would never forgive herself for the role she had played in all of that.

"No, I stayed home today." Abigail had just turned fifteen and had started lying a lot lately. Rather than call her on it, Margo decided to let it slide. The kids hated her enough right now.

"I kind of need some money." There it was, the reason for the call.

"Sure, Abby." It was her daughter's nickname from a long time ago, and Margo didn't seem to be able to stop using it, even though her daughter hated it now.

"Sorry, Abigail," she corrected herself. "How much do you need?"

"Like five hundred would be good."

It seemed like an awful lot of cash for someone her age and Margo's pulse beat faster as she thought of the possibilities.

"Can you tell me what you need the money for, honey?"

She was trying so hard to make up for the past, but it didn't seem to matter what she did. Her words and actions were always wrong. She hoped Abigail didn't catch on to her try-hard sickly sweet voice.

Abigail sighed loudly, and Margo knew that she had lost. Whatever the game was, she wasn't playing it right.

"Never mind. Forget it. I'll just ask Dad."

Margo had to calm herself every time the kids brought up David, and she held her breath before answering.

"No, I can help—" she started, but her daughter had already hung up on her. Margo looked at the time and shoved the last two bites of her sandwich in her mouth, drained the coffee, and decided that she would walk and talk.

She pressed David's name on her phone and waited for him to pick up. Her ex-husband was probably having a leisurely lunch somewhere with clients, drinking espresso and enjoying an overpriced meal in a trendy place with five-star food and service. The good life. The life they used to have together. Margo missed it. It had all slipped away so quickly.

Her call went to voice mail and Margo wanted to scream.

112

Of course he would screen his calls, especially hers. "Hey, asshole," she started her message, "what the fuck does my daughter need five hundred dollars for? Do you even know what our children are doing all day? Do you know that Abigail isn't in school right now? Get your worthless ass home and check on the kids, damn it!"

She pressed end call and stood outside the Laundromat for a moment. Her heart was pounding, and her blood seemed to boil in her veins. No matter what she did, it wasn't enough for Abigail and Thomas, and it seemed like David could do no wrong. Margo had lost them long ago and sometimes she felt like it would have been kinder if she had simply died instead of having her heart broken again and again.

She went inside and waved at Carol, the heavyset woman who worked the mornings.

"You're not going to believe what happened," Carol began.

She always wanted to give Margo the blow-by-blow account of the people that had been in, the minutia of what had happened. Margo had learned long ago to just set up her laptop in the back and start typing. Carol seemed to have less to say to the back of her head.

"Uh-huh," Margo said. She barely pretended to be interested but that was enough for Carol. She was oblivious to whether Margo listened or not.

She waved good-bye as her coworker walked out the door. It was time to start her third job.

Margo had been writing as a freelancer over the last year,

113

and it was the most lucrative job that she could find. In college, she always had her assignments written well ahead of their due dates. Writing had always come easy to her; she had a knack for it. Now she wrote term papers for spoiled college kids who would pass off her work as their own, that and anything else people wanted to pay her for. How could she blame people for a little plagiarism when she was a convicted felon?

Like what you've read?

CLICK HERE TO ORDER NOW

WAHIDA CLARK PRESENTS

Butterfly Bitch!

Sneak Peek

By
Wahida Clark & Michael A. Robinson

This is a work of fiction. Names, characters, places, and incidents either are the product of the author's imagination or are used fictitiously, and any resemblance to actual persons, living or dead, business establishments, events, or locales are entirely coincidental.

Wahida Clark Presents Publishing
60 Evergreen Place
Suite 904
East Orange, New Jersey 07018
1 (866)-910-6920
www.wclarkpublishing.com

ISBN 13-digit 978-1-944992-43-9 (print)
ISBN 13-digit 978-1-944992-44-6 (e-book)
ISBN   987-1-944992576 (Audiobook)
ISBN 978-1-944992620 (Hardback)
Library of Congress Cataloging-In-Publication Data:
LCCN 2014904049
1. transvestite 2. Thug Life 3. Thugs 4. Check Fraud
5. Life Sentence 6. Transgender 7. Drug dealers 8. African Americans-Fiction 9. LGBTQ

Cover design and layout by Nuance Art LLC
Book design by NuanceArt@aCreativeNuance.com
Proofreader Rosalind Hamilton
Sr. Editor Linda Wilson

Prologue

W ho's counterfeiting these checks?" the detective asked, sitting in a room filled with cigarette smoke.

"I don't know, I don't know." Peyton's whimpers worsened as the interview continued.

"Aw, give me a break with the sad girl act. You could be facing some serious charges that we could easily drop if you give up your source."

A smile appeared on Peyton's face once the detective said that. "You can drop the charges?"

"That's on the condition that you give us your source. We want to know who's making these counterfeit checks."

Peyton stopped her tears from falling. This was the hardest decision she'd ever have to make. But once made, she had to make sure that everything fell into place.

"Okay . . . Okay . . . I'll give you my source."

"When?" the detective asked.

"Please, can you give me a couple of days?"

The detective looked up at his partner who had just lit up another Marlboro. His partner nodded. "Sure, you got a week."

That's all she'd ever need.

* * * * * *

Summer almost missed the call she should have been expecting. It was no one other than her best friend.

She rushed to answer the phone. "Peyton?"

"Where are you? You should have been here."

"Hold your horses, bitch. I'm on my way." Summer hung up and washed her face after she finished brushing her teeth. She listened to Rihanna on her iPod, mouthing along to the song "Diamonds." Summer threw on a red spencer dress and some easy going flip-flops. One look in the mirror was all she needed to kick-start her day.

Breathtaking . . .

She flashed her porcelain smile, and she couldn't believe there was so much resemblance between her and her favorite artist Rihanna, except that she had more luscious measurements: 36-22-40; but lacked the colored eyes. The other thing she shared with Rihanna was the sex appeal.

It hadn't always been that way.

Summer hopped in her Range Rover truck that her uncle Kevin had bought her, and bee-lined it to Peyton's apartment across town.

Washington, DC at this time of the day had the worst traffic.

Peyton came out on the first honk of the horn wearing Michael Kors sandals with highlights of lime that went well with the lime green Bongo watch. She carried a cream Aldo bag. Candies' sunglasses hid her eyes. Summer's little white friend was fly. The graphic design Mill dress accentuated the soft touches of her curves.

"Come on, girl! We're running late," Peyton said.

"You need to hurry up and get your car out of the shop,"

119

Summer replied.

Peyton rolled her eyes. Their friendship had seen better days. Summer had, had a tragic breakup with Peyton's cousin, Clayton, who had beaten her nearly to death. Afterward, they just never had the same connection as friends.

Their photo shoot was in Hyattsville, Maryland. When they pulled up to the warehouse, a dark van swerved alongside Summer's truck as she parked, and three guys hopped out waving shotguns.

"Get out the truck, bitch!" one of the masked gunmen said as he leveled the double barrel shotgun in Summer's face.

It took everything in Summer's power not to faint, and she immediately started to sob. "I don't wanna die! Please don't kill me! I have some money in my purse!"

One of the other masked gunmen who was pulling Peyton around from the other side of the truck said, "Bitch, do you have eighty thousand dollars in your purse?"

"I'm gonna die!" Summer cried, realizing she only had $800 in her purse.

"Shut the fuck up!" the masked gunman yelled.

It only took seconds before Summer heard Peyton being smacked to the ground.

"Where's Ellis' money? You think you can play with somebody like Ellis? Bitch, you'll watch all your friends die first."

"I'm gonna get it," Peyton managed to say. But before she could finish, one of the masked gunmen was already flinging stuff out of Summer's purse. That was until he found Summer's ID.

"By midnight, if you don't have that eighty grand, I'm going to kill your girlfriend, and then tomorrow we'll find somebody else close to you to kill. Maybe your cousin, Clayton."

"No! Don't kill my friend."

"Well then, get that money!"

The masked man showed Sumner her own ID, as if she didn't believe he had it. With one last shove to the ground where Summer nearly lost her porcelain smile, the three armed gunmen hopped in the van and skirted off.

"I'm gonna die!" Summer kept saying through sobs. There was no way in hell that she could go through with her photo shoot. If those guys were telling the truth, they'd never have to worry about a photo shoot ever again.

Everything dawned on Summer as Peyton tried to hug her. She pushed her away but then tried to claw her eyes out. "They're gonna kill me because of you!"

Peyton was quicker than she looked. She jumped back and held her hands out in complete submission.

"Summer, wait! We can get the money. You know how to get the money. We can have it by nightfall." Peyton kept a fair distance as Summer neared her.

"I can't ask my uncle? I told you the situation between us."

"You know what I mean, Summer. We only have a little while left."

"You want me to cash some checks? Are you crazy! I

121

nearly died the last time when I almost got caught."

"You're my only chance."

"It's your own fault; all you do is gamble. I can't believe you went to a loan shark like Ellis. He would rather clean his books with bullets than to be owed."

"Help me please!" Peyton begged.

Summer went back to her Range Rover and sat down. She couldn't believe she was getting pulled into something she promised herself she'd never do again: bank fraud. But the more she saw the tears sprouting from her friend's eyes, and the promise of death lingering overhead, her decision was easy to make.

"Get in the car."

* * * * * *

Damn . . . Damn . . . Damn . . . Summer thought as she bee-lined it back to her apartment. She made one quick stop at Office Depot to get the specific set of checks she needed: payroll checks. She had been doing the scam for years until her tumultuous relationship with the love of her life, Clayton had come to an end, and she moved back to town.

But Summer didn't have any of her fraud ware on hand, and she'd have to go and get everything together.

She couldn't even look at Peyton as she got back in the truck after leaving Office Depot. The most she ever made cashing checks was eight to ten G's in one day. It was impossible in her mind to pull off ten times that much. But only if she could get enough good paper.

Summer stared ahead, but she told Peyton, "I'm gonna

drop you off at your apartment. Put on a nice, classy business suit and break out a briefcase. In about an hour, I'll come back and pick you up."

Peyton still had a shimmer of tears and a dash of fear in her eyes that lightened once she realized Summer would help her. "Thank you."

Summer took a deep breath. She couldn't be mad at her friend. "Don't worry. We'll have it by nightfall."

After leaving Peyton's apartment, she had to kick everything into gear. She had to get the account numbers from a guy she hadn't spoken to in six months, then go back to her apartment, make the checks, and then go and cash them. But there was a big glitch in her program. She didn't know if Glen, whom she hadn't spoken to in six months, would give her the account numbers. And that's why she was headed to her house instead of the bank.

She went into the house and quickly dressed in the sluttiest mini-dress in her closet. Then she put on foundation and the reddest lipstick she could find. Black eyeliner darkened her eyelids, and she pulled her hair into a neat ponytail. Damn, she needed her stylist, but this would have to do.

She kicked her flip flops off for a more seductive pair of Narcisco Rodriguez wedges that stuck her fine ass up for display, and then she headed straight for the door as she made the phone call she said she'd never make again.

Glen picked up on the second ring.

Summer was already hightailing it to his office, and it didn't matter what he said because by the end of the phone call she would have those much needed account numbers.

"What do you need, Butterfly?" His voice was flat, but after six months he didn't need her to ask or say anything to know she needed something.

"Glen . . . Hey. I wanted to call you because I haven't heard from you."

Glen smirked as he looked off to the side. He still wondered about Butterfly, who had all but pushed him away after he expressed his love for her.

"Are you still having nightmares?" Glen asked.

His inquiry was like a punch in Summer's gut. She figured he'd forgotten that. She'd been having them for as long as she could remember.

"I need to see you," she said, ignoring his question.

"Not now. I'm very busy." He couldn't have known that Summer was pulling up outside his law practice. She slid into the vacant parking spot next to his BMW and blatantly honked the horn. "Who the hell is that?" Glen asked.

"It's me," Summer said, putting the truck in park. She exited the vehicle and stood there so he could see her from his office window.

"I'll be out in just a second." They hung up as Summer laughed to herself.

"I thought so . . ." she said in an even voice.

It's true that Glen looked like a version of Eddie Murphy who had a serious bout with weight gain. He could dress nice, but the flopping love handles on his bad body threw everything off.

124

"I haven't heard from you in quite some time," Glen said, subdued by the lust egging at every ounce of his core.

"Glen, I'm really, really needing a really big favor," Summer said as she ran her fingers along his neckline and got closer and closer.

"I knew you needed something." He was almost about to break into a sweat. Summer was damn near breathing down his neck.

"I only need a dozen," she said as she slid her hand over his crotch area and gripped his dick.

"A dozen!" Even with her hand on his dick massaging it so pleasurably, the request was way beyond his limits. "I'll give you three."

"No!" Summer whined like a spoiled child. She pushed him on her truck and stuck her tongue down his throat.

"Okay, I'll give you five."

That still wasn't enough. She had calculated that the account numbers' figures would make a bit over eighty grand after she cashed them. But that would mean she'd need twelve checks to arrive at that amount. She knew what she'd have to do.

"Get in the backseat of the truck," she said.

Glen couldn't believe his ears. She briefly gave him some a year ago, but he had begged and begged for some more, but she never relented, using it as a carrot for a chasing horse.

He got in the back of the truck, and she followed him as she shut the door. Glen felt the pressure of his stiffened penis as she zipped his pants down and slammed his dick in her mouth.

"Oh God yes, Butterfly!" He sounded pathetic. It wasn't cries of pleasure, but admission of the love he still had for her.

Summer sucked on his dick as she looked at her watch. Fuck! It was nearly 12:00 p.m., and she still had to print the checks, get dressed, and pick up Peyton. She started to hum on his dick until he shot a wad down her throat that she gladly swallowed.

"Oh my god! I'm in love with you!" He kissed Summer's soft lips. How much longer would this have to take! It was unbelievable, but he was trying to undress her and his dick was still hard!

"Glen, I'm gonna give you some more tonight," Summer said in her most seductive way.

"I know, baby, but we're only at eight if you leave now."

Summer could have cursed under her breath, but she had to hurry and get twelve account numbers and skedaddle the fuck out of there.

"I ain't going nowhere until you fuck me in the ass and give me twelve."

"Oh baby, you're gonna give me some ass?" His lips were almost quivering with excitement.

"That's what I said I had for you." Summer didn't waste a moment. She spit amply on his dick and again in her hand as she pulled her mini-dress up and lubed up her ass. He was already groping away on her tits as she put her back to him and guided his medium size dick into her asshole.

"Oh fuck, Cla—" She almost slipped and said Clayton, but she corrected herself gracefully and said, "Glen. You feel so good." She hadn't fucked around in a minute, and it didn't feel good at all—it hurt like hell. But she slammed her hips back faster and faster until he was grunting and panting.

"Ahh—yes!" he uttered as he exploded. That time around, Summer had drained him completely. "Twelve . . . no—I'm gonna give you twenty." And that was that.

* * * * * *

Summer was back home in a flash. She looked at her watch. She had eighteen minutes left before she'd have to pick up Peyton. Her computer already had the software she needed to make the checks, so she entered the account numbers she had gotten from Glen, who in turn had gotten the account numbers from the accountant who worked at his firm. Summer pressed twenty copies each for all twenty account numbers.

While that was hatching, she ran to the shower and washed Glen off her and out of her and then dressed in a business skirt suit.

Time was ticking away.

She had to make the transactions during lunch hours, which was the busiest time of day. It would give her a higher chance that the bank wouldn't call on the checks to see if the people had written the checks out to her. But she knew if she didn't get a hold of herself, she would later regret it.

Summer took her medicine for her bipolar disorder and popped two Molly pills behind it. It was her favorite forbidden mix. After she made sure she looked decent, she grabbed the payroll checks off the laser printer and was out the door.

* * * * * *

Peyton was outside awaiting Summer's arrival. Peyton looked the part well enough. Since Summer had taken her meds and got fucked fast and hard in the ass, she didn't feel so hateful toward her friend.

"No time to waste. We have to cash these checks at their home branch. If they call on the check, leave immediately. We can go to the same banks and cash them together, but we have to hurry up and do this while it's lunch time." Summer explained every detail of the process.

Peyton flipped her eyes because she didn't need the pep talk. She had done this a thousand times, but she never learned how Summer got the paper. She still didn't know Summer's source.

Bank of America on M Street was their first stop. Each check was made out for eight G's, and if everything went according to plan, they'd be finished by the end of the lunch hour.

"You ready?" Summer asked.

"Yeah, I'm ready. I'm going to wait three minutes, and then I'll come in behind you."

"Okay. I'll see you then."

Summer went straight into the bank. Everything was going smooth. The guard standing at the door smiled at her and that always was a good sign.

As the line dwindled down to her, she noticed that Peyton still hadn't come in yet. Gosh, the bitch had to be faster on her feet, or they would never be finished by her timetable.

It was her turn . . .

Summer went to the bank teller, who was a female. That was always a bad sign. She should have allowed herself to be skipped until a male bank teller's counter became available.

Damn, shit wasn't adding up. And just then Summer remembered: she had forgotten to put super glue on her fingertips to cover up her fingerprints. *Shit!*

Everything in her mind told her to abandon this mission. But she couldn't just walk out with the threat of death hanging overhead. And shit! She didn't even have her ID anymore.

"Can I help you?" the easy-going bank teller asked.

Summer smiled kindly, and all her tension and uneasiness came off naturally.

"Yes. I'd like to cash this check."

"I'll just need your ID."

Of course, Summer thought. She fumbled through her purse and her wallet and lucky enough, her driver's license wasn't taken by the masked gunman. She always kept it behind her ID.

But still no Peyton anywhere in sight. *What the fuck!*

Summer laid her driver's license on the table to hear words that anybody who cashed checks illegally would hate to hear: "I'm going to have to check something real quick." If the bank teller called on the check, the owner of the check would

Wahida Clark & Michael A. Robinson

say they never made the check out to Summer, and she would be arrested on the spot.

Summer had to control this situation. "I'm really in a rush—my lunch break's almost up."

The bank teller studied Summer for a second. "Oh, forget about it. How would you like it?"

"Large bills," Summer said, and she could have kissed the lady as she cashed the check for eight thousand dollars. It brought back good memories of survival and making it finally out of the mud. "Thank you."

When Summer left out the bank, guns were drawn on her, and she fainted.

* * * * * *

"Bobby Moore, wake up," the detective said.

Summer awoke from her peaceful sleep. But when she saw the same detective who had put the gun to her head, she knew she wasn't having one of her recurring nightmares.

"Bobby Moore . . ." the detective chanted again and again, and Summer whose alias was Bobby Moore, couldn't believe the detective knew her real name.

Born a man, Bobby Moore had gone under the knife to add more bust to her bra-size, and had her ribs removed to make her waist seem slender. By taking butt shots, she tailored her figure until she had her desired results. The only thing left was to go all the way and have the sex change, which she put on hold after her break up with Clayton.

"I'll just die if I go to jail! They'll kill me in there!" Summer whose nickname was Butterfly, couldn't contain her

130

worst fears coming to life.

"Oh, you won't die. You have too much going for you," said the unkempt, fat detective, who smelled of deli pickles, bacon, and raw onions. Mustard stained his shirt and tie. Dark rings under his eyes didn't cover up the scattered moles, and his lips were too loose and gummy. Butterfly just hated him!

"You're going down!" the other detective said, who looked like a ridiculous version of ex-NBA baller, Jason Kidd, with his bushy eyebrows and slit lips.

"I can't. I'll die! I'll kill myself. Please don't take me to jail!" Butterfly begged, placing her hands in front of her face and noticing the handcuffs around her wrists. "Take these off, take these off! I promise I'll tell you everything."

The detectives smiled at one another. Why couldn't everybody be this easy?

"We have you on bank fraud, identity theft, counterfeiting and manufacturing—"

"Uttering forged documents," the other detective aided his partner's statement.

"You're going to get an enhanced sentence for sophisticated skills and a far lengthier sentence for the dollar amount," the Jason Kidd look alike said.

Butterfly heard nothing but her own sobs. How could her life continuously go deeper into a ditch? Wasn't it enough that she was born a man for crying out loud! There was no way she'd make it in a male prison. She'd be raped and passed around like reefer in a group of Rastafarians.

"Where did you get the account numbers from?" the

131

detectives asked, and before the words were off his lips, Butterfly said, "Glen! He gave them to me after I gave him some head and some butt!"

Notwithstanding Butterfly's distraught conditions, the detectives both broke down and laughed.

"It ain't funny!" Butterfly couldn't think of anything worse than being killed in prison by somebody who looked like Big Bubba on *Money Talks*. "I had stopped doing fraud, but my friend Peyton came to me because she owed Ellis, the loan shark, eighty grand, and I was only helping her out."

It all became clear to the detectives. They knew Peyton had set Butterfly up. But when they thought about Ellis the loan shark they laughed hysterically, because Ellis wouldn't loan money for gambling debts. From their investigation of that individual, he funded Black Market enterprises, not gambling debts.

"Get her the fuck out of here," the unkempt detective told the one that looked like Jason Kidd.

"I'm gonna kill myself," Butterfly said to the detectives.

"Get her, her medicine or tranquilize her ass."

She was being escorted to her cell at the DC jail, when she was sat down momentarily before being dressed out to don her prison garb. Moments later, Peyton came out of a room near Butterfly.

Peyton stopped right in front of Butterfly, and Butterfly wouldn't have noticed her through the lens of tears in her eyes until Peyton said sweetly, "Summer . . ." When Butterfly looked up, Peyton blinded her with a searing slap across her face. "Fuck you, you faggot bitch!"

* * * * * *

The following six months were a blur. Butterfly was heavily sedated during the whole ordeal in the DC jail. All she remembered was the frightening nightmares that tackled her in her sleep, and she'd scream herself into a corner of her cell and hug her knees to her breasts. She couldn't even remember her lawyer, or how he or the judge looked. The only thing she remembered was the judge finding mitigating circumstances to give her eighteen months in a medium security federal prison. She was being sent to FCI Schuylkill, PA.

During those six months, Butterfly only received one letter in the mail because she wouldn't tell anybody in her family that she was in jail.

Butterfly opened the letter to read the following:

Summer, Bobby, Butterfly, or whoever you think you are.

I finally was able to get you back for turning my family against me. You broke up our whole family because you never told me you were a "MAN" before I hooked you up with Clayton. Just know – Faggot . . . You TWISTED FREAK– that I got you in there. I set you up, sissy!

I hope you kill yourself in there, and if you don't have the courage to rid the world of one more fag, then I hope you get killed.

Just know, bitch, blood is thicker than water, and just because your family rightfully hates you for being a punk doesn't mean you have to [pervert] everybody else's. And since you're not even punk enough to own up to being a twisted man, you done got yourself tangled up in one of your twisted frauds. LOL. Get it: You faggot fraud.

If I ever see you again, I'm going to try to stick my 6" YSL's up your ass. Fuck, you'd probably like it, faggot! TWISTED-FREAK!

Butterfly was leveled. She ripped up the letter and flushed it down the toilet. Her inner shell was so weak, brittle, insecure and unsafe, that the smallest test could throw everything out of whack.

She grabbed the nearest razor, took out the blade, and deeply sliced both her wrists. The pain and the fear of death felt better than the pain from her life and the fear of going to prison. She climbed under her bunk until she fainted again.

Her cellmate found her and hit the panic button. Without that, Butterfly would have bled to death. She was placed on suicide watch until she made a full recovery, and then sent to FCI Schuylkill.

Chapter One
How Would She Survive!

Six months and a day and Butterfly was finally leaving DC jail. She was little more than a semblance of her former self. She had lost ten pounds and couldn't weigh more than a hundred and thirty pounds. Butterfly had lost her cinnamon color, and now she was high-yellow from not being exposed to the sun all that time in DC jail.

The US Marshals did all the transporting for the Feds. So after fifty or more inmates were cuffed and shackled, they were loaded on the transportation bus that everybody called the grey goose. The wee hours of Monday morning brought a cold breeze that left everybody shivering until they were on the heated bus.

"What you in for?" a Mexican asked Butterfly as he took the seat next to her. He wore dark D&G glasses that had to be corrective wear, or the DC jail wouldn't have let him have them. His mustache was perfectly trimmed, and his hair was slicked back.

Butterfly studied him for a few seconds, and she decided she wanted to talk. "Bank fraud."

"What are you? Dominican?" The more the Mexican talked the more Butterfly could tell that he had a sexy, heavy accent that was surprisingly easy to understand.

"No, I'm Black," Butterfly said. Notwithstanding the fact that she felt she looked like hell. But by the way she was being stared at because she could see nothing but raw hunger, and it told her she still looked good.

"Everybody calls me Sosa."

Despite Butterfly being filled with the fear of going to jail and having tried to kill herself not even three months ago, as well as her conflicting feelings about Peyton, Clayton, her uncle, and her family, it felt good speaking to Sosa.

"My name is Butterfly." A hint of a smile spread across her face.

"Mariposa," he seductively chanted in Spanish while licking his bottom lip. "Damn, I wish you were Mexican, or at least Spanish."

"What for?"

"Because I could have asked for you to be my cellmate. I just came from Schuylkill a year ago. I went back to Mexico, and the Feds came back and got me. Now I have a thirty year sentence." They were silent. Butterfly didn't know that he was the under boss of the biggest drug lord in Mexico, Chapo Guzman.

"But I own this pinche pais. You see, when I get back to Schuylkill, they're gonna make me shot-caller again. Ever since I've been locked down I've always called shots for my people. They got some nice names for shot-callers: they call us Reps or Representatives. Like we're running for Congress." They laughed. "But I spend lots of money every month." If Butterfly didn't know any better she would have thought he was over-exaggerating in the animated and excited way that he spoke. But she was so charmed by his charisma that she didn't notice it. "Every month," he continued, "I put $500 on ten different commissary accounts. I spend the shit like it's water."

Butterfly looked around to see if anybody was looking. It was still dark outside, being that it couldn't be any later than 5:45 a.m. Most everybody on the bus was asleep. "You must be rich."

"Listen to me." Sosa's accent was heavy and forceful. "I'm from Sinaloa. I know a lot of mero-mero. I think you call them Bosses. But listen, I want you to give me your name and register number."

"Register number?" Butterfly asked as she interrupted him.

"Yeah, it's the number everybody has in the federal prison system. Excuse my English; I think I'm saying it right." He organized the sequence of words in his head. "Yes, Federal prison system." He was pleased with himself, almost forgetting his train-of-thought. "Yes, I want your information."

"For what?" Butterfly was somewhat defensive, but elated that Sosa was so into her.

"I swear I gonna send you some money!"

Butterfly never had to accept money in exchange for sex. She had been kicked out of her father's house when she was seventeen years old, because her uppity father couldn't accept the fact that Butterfly was a pre-op transgender who was

137

going to have the operation to make Butterfly fully a woman once she turned eighteen. Her father lived under a pretense, being that he had a political career to uphold. He started off as a county commissioner in neighboring Hyattsville, Maryland, where he was eventually elected a seat in the state's legislation. All the annual banquets, monthly outings, balls, galas, and his fraternity conventions, and he never ever once brought Butterfly along—not once! She was always shuffled off neatly to her uncle Kevin, who had been molesting her ever since she was seven. And that's why she always associated the unfortunate sequence of words: Kevin-seven-heaven. Yes, Uncle Kevin was the pastor of one of the biggest Protestant churches in Maryland.

When Butterfly's father kicked her out, she was forced to live with her uncle, Kevin, who doled out money and lavish presents on Butterfly in exchange that she remain quiet about their daily sexual rendezvous. Uncle Kevin was sick to say the least, and insanely in love with Butterfly. He attributed his overzealous love to some farcical explanation of her being the "son" he never had—or couldn't have because his wife was infertile.

Butterfly could have told her father, but she knew 100% that her father would have killed Kevin, who was her mother Sandra's younger brother. So Butterfly always kept the fact that her uncle molested her a secret, and for the most part she kept the fact that she was a man a secret. Secrets . . . Secrets . . . Secrets.

Butterfly knew she had to leave her uncle's house. He was

138

becoming so increasingly in love with Butterfly that he became blatant with his affections toward her in front of his wife, Debra. He even kissed Butterfly on the lips once in front of Debra and would stay up in the furnished attic with Butterfly until the wee hours of the night.

Debra had been the owner of the franchise of women's clothing that she sold out of several different warehouses across the country called Debra's. She taught Butterfly the ins-and-outs of running a multi-million dollar franchise, but most importantly she taught Butterfly how to do payroll. It wasn't too long after that, that Butterfly used common sense to figure out how to counterfeit checks. And when she met her ex, Clayton, he had all the connection she'd ever need to obtain fake identification. At first, it was for the express purpose of identifying her as a woman, and secondly to cash checks!

"Why you haven't said anything? Did I offend you?" Sosa brought Butterfly out of her brief reverie. She had been crushed by the legal system, her family and friends, and depressed for as long as she could remember. So Sosa's smiling face was the least offending.

"No, I'm not offended," she said innocently.

"Then I send you money. I scared, 'cus you being morena."

"Morena?" Butterfly asked quizzically.

"Yeah." He laughed, not believing himself for going against all odds because he wanted to fuck Butterfly so much it hurt. "Morena means Black in Spanish. We also say Negra or Negro, but we don't say it because we think it will offend you."

"I'm not offended."

"I know, 'cus I not call you Negra. I say Morena. Morena deliciosa." They laughed. "See, I know you gonna cause mucho problema," Sosa said with charming and squinted eyes. It was a threatening foreboding prophecy that Butterfly couldn't exactly place, and it only exemplified what she had already feared.

"Why you say that?"

"You're gonna see, morena deliciosa. When those guys get one look at you, they're gonna get so hungry, they'll do anything to get some of you. I'd be able to smell you from the other side of that big compound. You smell so sweet I wanna fuck you right here."

They laughed again. Sosa couldn't be older than forty-five years old, but he still had a lot of youth.

"You're playing." She was hoping that was not the case, because she was non-confrontational. She wouldn't stand a chance if otherwise.

He laughed. "I no lie. I tell you this; those morenos from DC marry each other."

"Marry?"

He excitedly shook his head. "Once you get married, you married wherever you go."

Married! Good grief! Butterfly thought. She didn't know that it was a binding non-legal process equivalent to slaves hopping the broom. If she got married, wherever she would go, she'd be "whoever's" Mrs.

"I can protect you, morena deliciosa." Sosa's youthful and charming face was replaced by stern eyes that read: stone-cold killer. And his expression said the same. But no matter what he said in his last statement, there was only one thing Butterfly heard.

"I'ma need protection?" Butterfly asked, now visibly shaken as the sun finally cracked the horizon outside of the bus.

This time all the charisma and charm was all the way gone as Sosa looked over at her and nodded yes.

Like what you've read?

CLICK HERE TO ORDER NOW

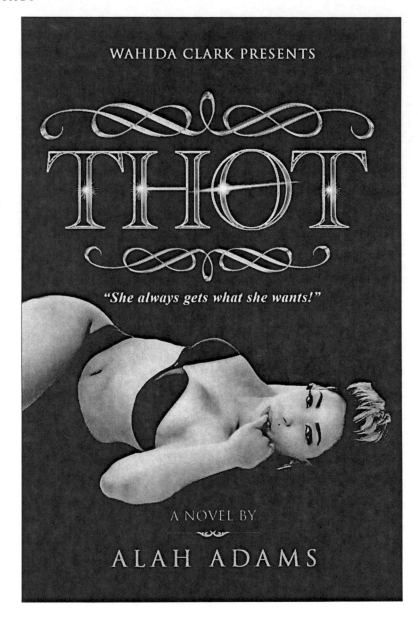

WAHIDA CLARK PRESENTS

T.H.O.T

BY

ALAH ADAMS

Wahida Clark Presents Publishing, LLC
60 Evergreen Place
Suite 904A
East Orange, New Jersey 07018
1 (866)-910-6920
www.wclarkpublishing.com

ISBN 13-digit 978-1-936649-25-9
ISBN 10-digit 193664925X
eBook ISBN 97819366490-6-8

Library of Congress Catalog Number 2017904229
1. Urban Life 2. Suspense 3. Drugs 4. Hustle, 5. New York City 6. African-Americans-Fiction 7.THOT

Cover design and layout by Nuance Art, LLC
Book interior design by www.aCreativeNuance.com
Contributing Editors: Linda Wilson and R. Hamilton

Printed in United States

Prologue

Vinny hid in the bedroom closet of the plush condo he purchased for Chasity. Heart racing with anxiety, he opened the bottle of Oxycodone he held and popped two pills. He shed tears as he listened to Torian pounding her vagina as if he were killing her.

"Oh my god!" Chasity screamed out in ecstasy. "You are the best! Keep fucking me!"

Furious, Vinny's chest heaved, and he couldn't control his jaw from grinding. His hand shook, almost causing him to drop his weapon and the pills. He shoved the bottle back into his pants pocket. *I can't believe this is happening. I trusted her with everything, and this is how she repays me.* Vinny cocked the .45 caliber ACP pistol. *I knew I should've listened to Rocco.* He sniffled. The effects of the powerful opiate was starting to kick in.

"What's that noise?" Torian asked, stopping mid-stroke after hearing a clicking of some kind. "Sounds like somebody's in the closet." Torian dismounted Chasity and grabbed his pants where he'd concealed his 9-millimeter. Before he could grip his weapon, Vinny rushed out of the closet busting shots.

Bang! Bang! Bang!

The first shot hit Torian in his shoulder, pushing him two

steps back. He fell to the floor about two feet from his 9-millimeter. He lay there not making a sound, pretending to be unconscious, yet inching his hand toward his gun. The other two bullets landed in the headboard right by Chasity's head.

"Vinny!" she screamed and flinched, holding her arms up in the air. "Baby, please put the gun down . . . It's not what it looks like."

"That's all you have to say!" He looked at her with red teary eyes, seething in anger.

Bang!

He let off a shot right by her head. Tears streamed down Vinny's face. "I gave you *everything!* I took you from living in motels selling your ass, to a condo and a BMW! And this is how you repay me!" He lunged toward her as if to strike her with the butt of his gun.

She quickly guarded her head with her hands. "Wait! I can explain!" She forced a smile in an attempt to calm him down.

"I don't want to hear it!" Vinny pointed the gun at Chasity. "I should kill you!"

Torian got his hand on his gun, but he didn't have a clear shot at Vinny because of the angle. Vinny moved closer to Chasity, putting the gun to her head, which gave Torian the perfect advantage. Just as Torian's index finger pressed on the trigger, Vinny saw him in his peripheral, turned, and let off two shots in rapid succession.

Bang! Bang!

One of the shots hit Torian in his chest, but not before Torian let off three shots at the same time. Two shots hit

Vinny in his neck; the third shot pierced the closet door. He slumped to the ground while gurgling on his blood. Both men lay on the floor, gravely injured.

Chasity stood viewing the carnage. Vinny tried to use his hands to squeeze the wounds in his neck to stop the blood from flowing. It was too late; in three minutes his hands unclasped his neck, and he lay peacefully still. Vinny was dead.

She slowly turned to look at Torian as he lay motionless with his eyes wide open staring right at Chasity. Instantly she turned her head and squeezed her eyelids as tight as she could. She opened them and turned back to the same horrific scene. The man she really loved was gone.

"This isn't real," she told herself. "Snap out of it!" She couldn't believe what had just happened.

At that moment, her mind had been stripped of its ability to reason. Disoriented, she gazed at both bodies as if they were illusions. Suffolk County police officers entering the room with their guns drawn, brought her out of her trance.

"Get on the floor with your hands behind your head!" the officer yelled.

Unresponsive, Chasity stood there stark naked.

The officer, seeing her blank expression, realized she posed no immediate threat. Cautious, he moved toward her, took one of the blankets that lay on the king-sized bed and covered Chasity's body. The other officers looked at the two bodies on the floor. They glimpsed the .45 caliber ACP next to Vinny, and the 9-millimeter lying next to Torian.

The first officer put his gun away and grabbed Chasity by her shoulders. "Miss, are you all right?"

She remained upright but in a catatonic-like state, experiencing the effects of extreme shock.

After a half hour, the officer took her to a police vehicle, while the homicide squad combed over the scene. It was cut and dry: two men shot each other to death over a woman. It didn't take long for them to surmise the situation.

Still in shock, but no longer catatonic, Chasity was escorted to the precinct where she was placed in a small interrogation room. The officer helped her put clothes on before they left. Now she sat in the cold, gray room looking confused. The door suddenly opened, and in walked a tall, heavyset female with a detective badge hanging from her neck. Her black pantsuit and white button-down shirt fit her frame well.

"How are you doing? My name is Detective Jennifer Colon." She wore a serious expression as she glanced at the paperwork she held. "Miss Chasity Tommyson, that's you, right?"

Chasity met the detective's gaze for a moment before turning her head and looking at the wall. She took a few seconds before speaking. "Yes, that's me."

"Okay, Chasity. Can you tell me what happened today?" Detective Colon slammed the door and looked down at Chasity with disgust. Her long, dark hair fell over her face, hiding her curled lip and heated gaze. She moved her hair aside and stared at Chasity with unfriendly dark brown eyes before taking a seat.

Chasity's eyes widened, but they didn't blink. She seemed to be regressing into her guilty conscience.

"Take your time, take a deep breath," Detective Colon suggested. "If you want me to help you, I need you to tell me how this happened . . . from the beginning."

Slowly, Chasity took in a deep breath and let it out just as measured.

"It all started a year ago when I first met Vinny . . ."

Detective Colon pressed record on the mini video recorder that sat on a tripod. "Okay, take your time. Start from the beginning."

Chasity closed her eyes, but when she opened them she began speaking. "I'm not at all what I appear to be. I have deceived many men by using my looks and my body to lure them into my world of lust. The warning signs were all around me, telling me to stop, telling me that there was danger ahead. But I didn't listen, and now two men are dead. And it's all because of me."

Chasity paused and gazed into the camera wearing a slight smile.

* * * *

CHAPTER 1

A Sucker, With a Capital 'S!'

Bay Shore Motor Inn
Bay Shore Long Island, New York

Chasity

" *Middle fingers up / throw them hands high / middle fingers up/tell em boy bye/boy bye/I aint thinking bout you/Sorry/naw I aint sorry."* Chasity sang along with Beyonce to her new single 'Sorry' as it blasted on the radio.

"This is my new anthem! Because I really don't give a fuck about these niggas!" Chasity spoke with passion while she inhaled a huge blunt, then she passed it to Kat.

"My sentiments exactly!" Kat replied as she reached for the blunt and inhaled.

Scantily clad in red Victoria's Secret matching bra and panties, Chasity sat on the bed with her laptop open, checking her traps on the infamous "Front Page" website. Front Page was a way for tricks and 'hos to link up via the Internet. She liked to use the word *trap* to describe the way she enticed weak men into her web of deceit and pleasure. Chasity was a modern day call girl, a prostitute, otherwise known in the hood as a THOT, an acronym for 'That Ho Out There.'

"The day just started, and I already have three new traps lined up. At $250 apiece, that's $750 for about an hour's worth of work," Chasity said to Kat, her best friend and partner in crime.

"The way these tricks be coming so fast, you can cut that hour into thirty minutes worth of work." Kat inhaled the blunt and then passed it to Chasity.

"I got this one trick that fucks me for the whole hour! I think that nigga be on something before he comes here," Chasity responded.

The days of 'hos walking the strip trying to catch a date were a thing of the past. Nowadays these young thots knew how to use the Internet to their advantage by posting provocative pictures with an implied message. The tricks were up on the new technology, so they went on the sites looking for new 'hos to trick on. That cut out the pimp and the risk of being seen by detectives walking on the 'Thot Trot,' the blocks where primitive thots walked trying to catch a trap.

Chasity and Kat were two of the best 'thots' in Long Island. Both women were voluptuous with gorgeous faces. They were divas, so they always adorned their heads with expensive wigs, kept their toes and nails done, and wore the newest designer labels. They were known to frequent the VIP section in the hottest clubs, buying their own bottles, balling out!

Tall with big brown eyes, Chasity inherited a honey-brown complexion from her Puerto Rican mother and black father. Her pearly white teeth were esthetically pleasing to the eye. When she got dressed up, people often told her she resembled Beyoncé. She kept her stomach flat which made her firm, size 38D cups stand at attention. Chasity was a complete ten!

Kat was a bit shorter, but her ass wasn't. Ass for days, flat stomach, and a nice amount of tits, she was a little darker than Chasity, but people always mistook them for sisters. Chasity and Kat didn't see the resemblance, but they chalked it up to them being around each other so much that they started looking alike. As a team, they were like the dynamic duo.

"That's my number one trap texting me," Kat said when her phone went off. "He's here. I'm going to my room to take care of him."

"Okay, my trap should be here shortly. I'll see you for lunch," Chasity said.

"That sounds like a plan."

Kat went two rooms down. They always got rooms close to each other for safety. Being that they didn't have pimps to protect them, they both kept revolvers close to them at all times. In the past, they had been violated by tricks who knew they didn't have pimps.

Shortly after Kat left the room, Chasity's new trap

knocked on the door. She knew it was him, so she sprayed herself with Chanel No. 5 before answering. Her motto was "Go above and beyond to please" to ensure that her traps stayed loyal. She answered the door in her Victoria's Secret undergarments.

"Hi. Vinny, right?" she asked, showing her perfect rows of white teeth.

"Yes, I'm Vinny. You're Cherry?" he asked in a nervous tone. *Wow! This chick is fucking beautiful! I hit the jackpot!* Vinny was stuck in thought standing in the doorway.

She quickly glanced at him from head to toe before inviting him in. "You can come in and make yourself comfortable."

Short, fat, and Italian with slick, black hair, Vinny wasn't quite the looker, but he was very charming. He possessed a gentleman-like quality that made him attractive to women. He was like a knight in shining armor, without the shining armor.

Chasity had a sixth sense for men who were enamored by her. Her 'sucker for love' meter dinged off the charts with this new guy. At first sight she could tell he was smitten by her beauty. She was a pro at tempting men, so she knew exactly how to handle him.

"So, Vinny, what do you do for a living?" she batted her light brown eyes.

"I'm in the construction business." Vinny stared at her in awe.

"Oh, I see . . . construction. Are you a foreman?" she

asked.

"No. I own a construction business with my family." Vinny kept rubbing his hands together in an attempt to calm his nerves. *Get it together, Vin!* he thought.

"It must be nice to work with your family."

"Not all the time, but it beats working for some Joe Schmo."

Chasity stared in his eyes and he got weak. She moved closer and he almost jumped. Normally, she would ask for money up front, but she was playing him all the way to the bank. She smelled money like a shark smells plasma.

"Relax, I'm not going to bite you. Unless you tell me to." She smiled, and Vinny seemed to unwind a bit.

Getting right down to business, Chasity unbuckled his belt and pants and pulled his penis out. Vinny almost freaked out, breathing heavily. Immediately, she took him into her mouth as if her life depended on it. The force with which she sucked his penis made Vinny's toes curl in seconds. She felt his sperm swelling up in his balls early, so she slurped with more ferociousness.

"Oh my God!" Vinny yelled out in ecstasy. "I'm coming!"

"Mmmmm! It tastes so good!" Chasity said as she lapped up his semen.

Vinny's eyes rolled around in his head. "You're the best! I mean that."

"Never had any complaints."

"No, really. No woman has ever made me come that fast from sucking my dick before." Vinny took out five 100 dollar bills. "I know you said it was only $250, but you were so good I'm giving you double!"

I got him! Hook, line, and sucker! "Aww, you don't have to do that. You're so sweet, Vinny."

"No, I want you to take it. I want to see you every day if that's possible?" He panted as sweat beads dotted his forehead and nose, looking at her like a puppy that needed attention from its master.

"Of course you can, silly!" Chasity laughed. "You're so funny!"

". . . Can we just cuddle for a minute?" Vinny knew that was a weird question.

"Sure, baby. Take your clothes off and get under the covers. You still have about fifty minutes left."

Vinny did as he was told. He curled up and went to sleep with Chasity as if she were his wife. He was officially open.

Damn this nigga hooked already, and I didn't even throw this tight, wet pussy on him yet. Chasity let him sleep for an hour, then she woke him.

"Wake up, sleepy head. Time to go."

"Damn, I was out of it." Vinny got up and put his clothes on. "So, I'll see you tomorrow at the same time?"

"If that's what you want, honey. I'll be here waiting for you, baby." She kissed him on the cheek.

Vinny finally left, and she watched him walk away to see what model car he drove. When he sat comfortably in a new jet black BMW 650i convertible, she knew she'd hit the jackpot. *Everything about Vinny screams money. And I want it all!*

Just as Vinny was leaving, Chasity got a text from her next client: *I'm pulling in right now.*

Chasity: *Okay, I'm ready.*

She went to the bathroom and rinsed her mouth out with mouthwash and brushed her teeth. As she was finishing up, there was a knock on the door.

With the same smile as before, she answered it. "Hi, Tommy. Come in and make yourself comfortable."

Tommy was a regular, and he wasn't a two-minute man. He was smart enough to pop a Viagra before his weekly appointments. Also, Tommy wasn't rich. He was just a truck driver with an appetite for young thots. Every week he would spend his hard earned money on one hour of pleasure.

Tall and light-skinned, the older black man had been married twice and divorced twice. Although he came equipped with a ten-inch penis, his last girlfriend cheated on him with his best friend, and that's when he decided to deal with women like Chasity and call it a day. For him it was less headaches and no commitment, that's what he enjoyed most about the situation.

Tommy didn't waste any time. Chasity knew that Tommy came to put in work, so she prepared her mind for the task of getting fucked hard. He took his clothes off and put his stiff penis in her mouth and shoved it down her throat. She moaned in protest, but she didn't stop him from manhandling her. There was something about his roughness that Chasity enjoyed. He didn't treat her like the doll she appeared to be.

Tommy treated her like the thot he knew she was. And Chasity loved it.

For fifty-five minutes straight, Tommy pummeled her vagina before ejaculating and leaving her sore. "I'll see you next week, same time." Tommy was a man of few words. He was dressed and out the door minutes after he was done.

Chasity had twenty minutes before her next appointment, and she wasn't ready. She dragged her sore body to the bathroom and took a long, hot shower. As she rubbed her vagina, she thought about her first trick, Vinny. *I knew Vinny was a breadwinner! What if I can entice Vinny to the point where he'll just take care of me, and I don't have to be fucking like this for money? It would be nice to be taken care of for a change.* She became so engrossed in her thoughts that she lost track of time.

There was a knock on the door. Her next trap was on time.

"Hold on, I'm coming!" she shouted from the shower as she got out and dried off. *Got to get this money. It's all in a day's work.* Chasity opened the door.

"Hi Paul. Come in and make yourself comfortable."

The quick arm movement in her peripheral disrupted Chasity's recollection. Detective Colon paused the video. "So, you met Vinny on the Front Page website." A beat passed before she spoke again. "I'm going to do you a favor."

"What's that?"

"I'm not going to arrest you for prostitution. Let's just pretend like I don't know anything about that. I'll erase the whole first part when we're done, so we both won't get into hot water."

Detective Colon pushed record on the video. "Continue." *Murderous slut! You just couldn't keep your fucking cunthole closed!*

Like what you've read?

CLICK HERE TO ORDER NOW

WAHIDA CLARK PRESENTS

H E A T

A NOVEL BY

MECCAGLOBAL

This is a work of fiction. Names, characters, places, and incidents either are the product of the author's imagination or are used fictitiously, and any resemblance to actual persons, living or dead, business establishments, events, or locales are entirely coincidental.

Wahida Clark Presents Publishing
60 Evergreen Place
Suite 904A
East Orange, New Jersey 07018
1(866)-910-6920
www.wclarkpublishing.com

Library of Congress Cataloging-In-Publication Data:

HEAT/ by MECCAGLOBAL
ISBN 13-digit   978-1-936649-13-6 (paper)
ISBN: 978-1-936399-42-0 (e-book)
•   ASIN: B01DOEI5T6 AUDIOBOOK
LCCN 2014916391

1.   Fiction- 2. Newark, NJ- 3. Drug Trafficking- 4. African American-Fiction- 5. Urban Fiction   6.thug life

Cover design and layout by Nuance Art, LLC
Book design by Nuance Art, LLC –
NuanceArt@aCreativeNuance.com
Edited by Linda Wilson
Proofreader Rosalind Hamilton

Printed in USA

CHAPTER 1

Order to Kill

~Flashback~

January 1, 2000

"W" e gon' show motherfuckers what happens when they steal from us!" Will shouted into the phone.

"Yo, what's up, Mike?" Samad asked curiously, with the cell phone pressed to his ear. He sat at a stop light in a red BMW with the top down. "What's goin' on?"

"This Will, boss man. It's done. We kidnapped some of them niggas that stole from us. We got 'em here at the warehouse."

"Good. Everything is going according to plan. Did y'all follow every detail down to a tee?"

"Yeah. We set up a fake drop-off and pick-up to get them niggas here. They thought they were meeting somebody else. Then they lookin' all surprised when we show up."

"Don't let none of 'em get away," Samad said.

"They won't make it out of this warehouse alive. Especially ya man, Eli."

"Good. Keep that thieving ass nigga breathin'. I want my face to be the last one he sees before he goes to hell. I'm gon' make him an example for other crews. It'll teach people what happens when they steal from me, or try to take over my territory. We need to send a message to all these brave niggas out here. I'm on my way." Samad ended his call, tossed the phone in the passenger seat, then sped to the location with murder on his mind.

Ten minutes later, he walked in the warehouse door with both guns drawn. A dead body lying on the ground with no head attached snatched his attention. *What the . . .*

Loud voices came from the far end of the hallway. He tipped through the hall listening for intruders and braced himself against the wall when he heard footsteps approaching.

A tall, dark-skinned guy turned the corner and ran right into the barrels of both guns. Startled, he cursed before putting his hands up in surrender mode and slowly backing away. The frightened young man continued backing up, even around the corner in the direction he ran from. Samad followed.

"Please don't shoot," the helpless young man begged. "I got a daughter and a son at home."

Samad put his guns down slowly, sensing the man's instant relief. But Mike's .40 caliber was drawn and ready to shoot his head off. Samad leaned on the wall and watched the guy turn, coming face to face with Mike.

"Nooooo! Please don't shoot!" the guy yelled.

"Happy New Year, motherfucker!" Mike fired the pistol twice. The young man's body made a loud thump as it hit the floor.

"Where's Eli?" Samad asked.

Mike gestured with his head to indicate he was down the hall. "I left him with Will."

"Ay yo! Stop him! He's tryna escape!" Will suddenly yelled, his voice echoing throughout the warehouse.

A dark figure cut around the corner and collided with Samad and Mike. All three men stumbled, but quickly gained their balance. Eli stopped in his tracks when he saw Samad. They stared at one another for a split second. Will rushed toward them with his 9-millimeter cocked.

"Don't shoot him!" Samad ordered.

A bullet exploded from the chamber. The blast ripped through Eli's back, causing him to fall flat on his face.

Eli's blood splattered on Samad's jeans. Samad looked down at himself then took a step back.

"Why the fuck you shoot him before we get the info from him!" Samad shouted.

"He was trying to get away!" Will replied.

"I needed to know where he hid the money he took from my other stash house." Samad glared at Will. "Before he took his last breath, I wanted that snake to watch the video footage of him sneaking out my spot. So he could know why he was about to die! He didn't know I had cameras, and I saw him with my own eyes. He also got some important papers I need."

"Damn, I ain't know all that, Samad," Will said.

"I know you didn't because this was before me, you, and

Mike linked up and started gettin' money. He was fuckin' around with my ex, and she trusted him, not knowin' Eli was one of my enemies. But *he* knew who *she* was. So one day he set up a break-in at the house and got away with a lot of money and paperwork out the safe. Lucky we wasn't home."

"My bad, boss," Will added.

"A lot of valuable stuff was stolen," Samad said, looking directly at Will. "He got a lot of shit that belong to my ex girl Keisha. Her brother's comin' home from jail next year too. I know he would want her personal things. I mean, he still got the safe deposit keys to the lock boxes."

"Like the lock boxes they have in a bank?" Mike asked.

"Yeah. Insurance papers are in there naming me as her beneficiary too."

"Straight up?"

"Yeah. We were gonna get married, so we was tryna get shit in order. Around that time she inherited some serious money from her father. But that's why I need to get my hands on that stuff."

"I understand," Will said. "My bad for real."

Samad stared at the blood leaking out of Eli. "He just got a lot of important paperwork from my old lady, and I need it.

"Damn, Samad . . . I ain't know."

"I'm just gonna have to go a different route to get it now. Maybe his girl knows something. But from now on, wait until I give you the order to kill!"

Will clicked the safety on his gun. Samad shook his head and turned his attention to Mike.

165

Mike glimpsed movement from Eli. "Yo, he still alive!"

Eli put his hand in his pocket, as if reaching for a gun. Mike aimed his gun at his head. Eli grabbed his phone and tried speaking, but he coughed up blood and gurgled.

Samad moved closer to the blood pooling near Eli's side. "He's done, Mike."

Finally, Eli took a deep breath before dying with his phone in his now limp hand.

Samad, Mike, and Will stood over his lifeless body. "Whoever he was tryna call must've been important," Mike joked.

"Or he was tryna warn a nigga," Will said.

"It is what it is, but that'll teach 'im about stealin' from me!" Samad said.

"And anybody else who even thinks about crossin' us!" Mike added. Will nodded in agreement.

Samad kneeled and went through Eli's pockets. He took the phone from his hand and looked at the display. "Born?" he said, glancing at Mike and Will.

"Born?" Samad said the name again. "I know this nigga Eli not workin' with my so-called homie, Born!"

Mike, Will, and Samad stared at each other, letting Born's name sink in.

"It's clean up time, boss man," Mike finally said. "C'mon Will. We got work to do." The two soldiers dragged the other two bodies to the center of the room.

Samad grabbed a metal can from the warehouse floor and poured gasoline on the bodies, then lit a match. The 'whoosh'

166

of the fire backed all three men up as the fiery flames spread, burning the bodies.

Mike, Will, and Samad picked up the duffel bags full of coke and the briefcases filled with money and exited the side door.

"Y'all know his peoples gone be looking for him, right? The streets gon' be talkin' up a shit storm," Will said.

"Let 'em talk. I don't know shit. Ain't heard shit, aint see shit," Mike responded.

"Dead men tell no tales. I'll meet y'all at the trap spot," Samad said, heading to his car.

An hour later, Samad sat inside the trap house watching the money counter as it came to a halt. His eyes widened as he read the numbers. "Three hundred thousand!"

"Betcha Eli won't be touchin' nobody else skrilla!" Mike said, sitting across from Samad.

"I hope that dirty nigga burn in hell!" Samad said evenly.

Mike stood and stretched, letting out a loud sigh. "Whoo wee! Three hundred g's sound lovely. Man, listen, it's about to be on! Competition is dead! Nobody gettin' it like we gettin' it! They gotta come to us!"

"Word!" Will agreed.

"Ten kilos of pure, uncut Columbian coke!" Mike and Will both said as they tossed a few kilos to Samad.

"Now it's time to take over every spot. Drop the price, and get richer than we are. Making sure everybody on this team eat. Fuck the competition!"

He caught the coke and smiled with greed in his eyes. "It's

on!"

Like what you've read?

CLICK HERE TO ORDER NOW

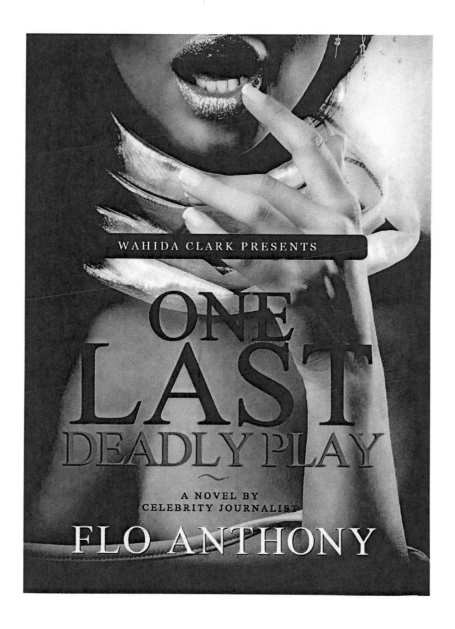

WAHIDA CLARK PRESENTS

One Last Deadly Play

A Novel By
FLO ANTHONY

This is a work of fiction. Names, characters, places, and incidents either are the product of the author's imagination or are used fictitiously, and any resemblance to actual persons, living or dead, business establishments, events, or locales is entirely coincidental.

Wahida Clark Presents Publishing, LLC

60 Evergreen Place

Suite 904

East Orange, New Jersey 07018

1(866)-910-6920

www.wclarkpublishing.com

ISBN 13-digit 978-1-936649-05-1

ISBN 10-digit 19366490550

eBook ISBN 9781936649198

Library of Congress Catalog Number

1.   Urban, Romance, Suspense, Gossip, Football, New York City, African-American, Street Lit – Fiction

Cover design and layout by Nuance Art, LLC

Book interior design by www.aCreativeNuance.com

Contributing Editors: Linda Wilson and R. Hamilton

Printed in United States

171

Chapter One

Columbus

Columbus wished he had a clue to his true identity or where he really came from. The sole doctor on Crooked Island told Columbus that he suffered from something called "traumatic amnesia," a condition that must have occurred as a result of his near drowning. Some fishermen, who are part of the 350 residents on the island, pulled him out of the ocean half a decade ago. Since he had no recollection of ever even having a name, the guys decided to call him Columbus Isley after Christopher Columbus, who sailed down the side of the island in 1492.

Christopher Columbus called the island the Fragrant Isles. Legend said it was because of the refreshing scent of the cascarilla tree's bark, also called Eluethera bark. Thus, he had been named Columbus Isley, with his surname deriving from Isles. One of the fishermen who rescued Columbus said it was the last name of a famous singing group made up of brothers in the United States. Columbus couldn't remember having any brothers, but he did have a vague feeling that he had known a couple of men who looked like him.

As he'd done each and every morning at the crack of dawn for the last five years, Columbus Isley prepared breakfast for the guests at Morning Glory, a small lodge with only twelve

172

rooms. He fingered the sparkling bottle-like emblem that hung from a thick gold chain around his neck after cracking the last egg. His friends had explained that it was a replica of a bat used to play an American game called baseball. The lodge provided only one television inside the bar, and it only got six local stations, so Columbus still had no idea what the game was. There was nothing even vaguely familiar about it to him.

Aside from the few tourists who actually traveled to the secret community located 583 miles off the Florida coast and the residents on the island, Columbus hadn't had much contact with the outside world. Only one telephone was in the lodge's office, and most residents depended on generators for electricity. There was no use of credit cards and only one bank. The mail boat came once a week, and only one flight arrived and departed twice weekly at Colonel Hill, a 4,000-foot airstrip on the southwest portion of the island.

Columbus, a black man with skin the color of honey and wild, curly, salt and pepper gray hair, piercing green eyes and the body of an African warrior, managed to catch the eye of a twenty-three-year-old white woman who originally came to Crooked Island accompanied by an addiction coach to overcome a problem with heroin. She also wanted to escape the fast-paced, drug-fueled modeling world in New York City and get her life and mental and physical well-being back.

Over the past couple of years, Ariel and Columbus had become very attached. One thing he remembered was how to make love to a woman, and how good his penis felt every time he entered her vagina. Just thinking about Ariel made Columbus's loins throb. He smiled. His lady was due back on Crooked Island on today's plane. Soon, they would be lying on a secluded beach, lost in a sea of lust.

His thoughts must have conjured her up. As Columbus got the coffee going, two milky-white arms wrapped around his waist. The beautiful woman's delicious smelling perfume engulfed him. He turned, pulled her to him, and then deeply kissed Ariel Pembrough, a bootylicious blonde with skin soft to the touch.

"You're back," Columbus said with a grin.

"Yes, I am," purred the supermodel, as her sky blue eyes glittered up at him. She stepped out of her yellow maxi sundress. She was panty-less.

Quickly locking the kitchen door, Columbus lifted her up on the counter and spread her legs. In the heat of passion he pulled his shorts down, then thrust his manhood into Ariel. These two lovers became one, losing themselves into each other.

"Well, that was a nice welcome," said Ariel as Columbus gently wiped her clean with a warm cloth as if she were a baby. She slipped her dress back on. Kissing her lightly on the lips, Columbus noticed the newspaper sticking out of her purse.

"What are you reading?"

"Oh, just an article about this wild murder case that's about to go on trial in Los Angeles today. It caught my attention because the guy in the photo looks like a lighter version of you. I thought he could be related to you or something. It says his name is Rolondo Jemison. It also involves the gossip columnist, Valerie Rollins. She's a friend of my mom's." Both names jarred something in his head. Columbus looked at the picture of the man. Sharp pains made him think his head was about to explode. A massive pounding in his chest quickly followed.

"Arrghhhh," he groaned as he collapsed on to the floor.

Like what you've read?

CLICK HERE TO ORDER NOW

WAHIDA CLARK PRESENTS

THUGGZ VALENTINE

BY
WAHIDA CLARK

Wahida Clark Presents Publishing
60 Evergreen Place
Suite 904A
East Orange, New Jersey 07018
1(866)-910-6920
www.wclarkpublishing.com

Library of Congress Cataloging-In-Publication Data:

Thuggz Valentine by Wahida Clark
ISBN 13-digit   978-19366496-3-1 (paper)
ISBN 10-digit   1936649632 (paper)
ISBN 13-digit   978-1-936649-18-1
ISBN 10-digit   1-936649-18-7
LCCN: 2015910467

1. New Jersey- 2. Thug Life 3. Murder- 4. African American-Fiction-
5. Urban Fiction- 6. Natural Born Killers-
7. Gangster Disciples- 8. Prescription Drugs- 9. HIV- 10. AIDS-

Cover design and layout by Nuance Art, LLC
Book design by www.aCreativeNuance.com
Sr. Editors Linda Wilson, Latoya Smith and Keisha Caldwell
Proofreader Rosalind Hamilton

Printed in USA

THE END
Bless and Ebony

CHAPTER ONE

February 14

6:15 p.m.

T huggz Valentine, mutherfuckaz!"
The ground shook from the explosion.

Kabooooooom!

The blast rattled the ground like an earthquake, igniting cars and SUVs, shattering store windows, knocking out the power, and setting off car alarms within a two-block downtown Newark radius. Several bystanders were killed, including a few police officers who'd had the two suspects surrounded, as well as every person inside the overturned bus, which was the source of the blast. People thought it was a terrorist attack.

It wasn't.

It was a standing ovation for Bless and Ebony. They embraced death on their own terms. They lived their last day on the edge and to the fullest. Even though it was filled with murder and mayhem.

Three minutes earlier . . .

6:12 p.m.

"Fuck y'all!" Bless managed to yell out, despite the burning sensation of the bullet wounds and a natural sense of impending doom. His head rested on Ebony's lap while her back leaned against the underbelly of the overturned bus.

Ebony stroked his head. "Shhh baby. Save your energy."

Muffled cries and yells of anguish echoed from the passengers trapped inside. There was no escape. The bus had landed on the door side, destining everyone inside to a fiery fate. Desperate, the imprisoned riders beat furiously on sealed windows, too dazed and hurt by the crash to even come close to shattering them. Their hysterical eyes gazed at all the police surrounding them in a half moon formation. Officers shielded themselves behind open doors with automatic weapons, pistols, and shotguns all trained on Bless and Ebony. High above, a police helicopter hovered.

"It's over." Bless closed his eyes.

"No, baby, not yet. Remember what you said? Real gangstas never give up," she reminded him.

He forced a smile onto his lips. "You . . . you, could've saved yourself."

With tears running down her cheeks, she stroked his face. "Today has been the best day of my life. Before you, I didn't know what it really meant to be free. I am feeling totally alive. Anything after this would be a disappointment. I love you, Bless," she expressed, but she knew he hadn't heard her. She

181

felt his body convulse, tighten, and then relax. She knew he was gone. She had been speaking to his soul. A soul she knew much deeper than even she was conscious of. Ebony held back every tear but one, which escaped down her cheek. She closed Bless's lifeless eyes with two fingers that resembled the peace sign, and then laid her gun on her leg. A tall, black detective stepped out of the police mob with his arms raised. He advanced slowly.

"Listen to me, Miss. Please. This can all end peacefully. I want to walk you out of this alive," he pleaded.

"Believe me . . . I plan to," Ebony said.

"That's good. Very good," he replied, missing the significance of her tone.

Ebony reached into Bless's pocket and pulled out his crumpled pack of Newport's and matches. "Don't shoot! Don't shoot! It's just a cigarette!" she bellowed at the itchy trigger-fingered officers.

Just a cigarette . . . She didn't smoke.

She put it in her mouth, lit it up, then inhaled a satisfying stream of smoke. When she exhaled, all the fear that she was harboring vanished.

"Now, I'm going to ask you to toss the gun over, okay?"

She inhaled. "Not yet."

He shook his head. "No! I said now! Look around you."

She did.

"It's over! There is nowhere to go!" he warned her.

Ebony glanced at all the stone-faced police squinting through scopes, with her head in the crosshairs. She took in all the gawking downtown onlookers, all while hearing the stifled cries of the people on the bus. And lastly, she looked up at the beautiful blue sky.

"Yeah, you right. There's nowhere to go . . ." she remarked, and then struck another match. "But up."

She and the cop exchanged glances. Yet, he strained at the match. The realization hit him when he saw the leaking gas from the overturned bus pooling in the street and settling like a beached whale. His brown eyes widened in horror, taking in the implications of the lit match.

"Nooooo!" hc yelled.

But it was too late . . .

"Thuggz Valentine, mutherfuckaz!" she screamed, laughing as if life was one big joke.

Then . . . she tossed the match.

Like what you've read?

CLICK HERE TO ORDER NOW

CPSIA information can be obtained
at www.ICGtesting.com
Printed in the USA
LVOW07s2057221017
553343LV00001B/2/P